A SMALL TOWN CAN BE #MURDER

JULIE SEEDORF

ISBN: 978-0-578-60548-7

Published by Skye Bridge Publishing

Printed in the United States of America

Cover art by Dp Photography

ACKNOWLEDGMENTS

I would like to thank Skye Bridge Publishing and my editor, D.A. Sarac. I am grateful for Timya Owen, Pat Dennis, Diane Weiner, and Sharon Mierke for their reviews and honest feedback. It always makes a writer better when they listen to those who have wisdom with the writing process.

My friends Donna Swenson and Sandy Coats encourage me every day to be better and to not give up when I doubt myself. Thank you. I consider myself blessed to have these people in my life.

Local photographer David Paal not only added to my book cover but gave me ideas for my creative mind and story. I am privileged to have been part of this project.

This book is for my father, Jessie Young.
His memory lives forever in my soul.

My dedication extends to my Wells, Minnesota, community and my readers,
who without them I wouldn't have a platform for things dear to my heart.

CONTENTS

INTRODUCTION

Excitement fills my soul when I start a new series. The Whistle Stop series takes a slight turn from my other works in that it is a bit more serious in places, touching on subjects close to my heart. I took a risk with these subjects not usually seen in cozies. As cozy authors, we want our books to take us away to magical places. Though our lives are magical at times, we also have to learn how to manage the in-between that pulls us down and presents us with unforeseen predicaments.

#A Small Town Can Be #Murder takes place in a small town somewhat like what I grew up in and still live in today. It wasn't until I got older that I appreciated what a small community offers- a family that is not related by blood. We nitpick, we complain, we spy on our neighbors, and we feel isolated at times. But there is nowhere else

where you want to be in times of trouble. When I had surgery for a broken leg and was confined to my bed for six weeks, the community rallied around and I was never alone. I didn't make a meal for six weeks. My husband had previously lost a job and started a new one and couldn't take time off, so this community took care of us. People I didn't know gave of their time to do many kindnesses for us. Recently a young boy living in this community was diagnosed with cancer, and the entire town supported him and his family through his journey. Another neighbor couldn't afford to paint and upkeep their house. Volunteers from this community took on the project. This story is told time and time again in small towns all across America. Small towns are family.

One of the things I like to do in each book is bring something from my past into my writing. This time it is the White House Eatery and the Wells Depot (shown on the cover). Growing up, we ate at The White House Café, a structure on Main Street. It was a large white nondescript building, but it is well-remembered in our community still today for its good food and friendliness by the owners. The building no longer stands, but its legacy will live forever.

I chose Whistle Stop as a name for my small town because my community was built around the railroad and I lived by the railroad tracks and watched the trains. I have many hobo stories. The old depot is now the Depot Museum, and the railroad legacy lives on, along with the trains that still travel through our town. Let me tell you... the whistle is loud. I have included a little history about the depot at the back of the book.

Although this book is fiction, some of my characters are named after people in my life I love, such as my dad Jessie or my son Matthew, though their characters bear no resemblance to them in real life.

I hope you enjoy visiting Whistle Stop, Minnesota. There is nothing greater than growing up and living in a small town. Oh, and this cozy will still give you a warm fuzzy.

Julie Seedorf

CHAPTER ONE

"While reading that old history book of our town, did you discover that Orvis the ghost haunts the lake house and blows watery kisses from the lake when a pretty new woman visits the area?"

Angel Delaight looked up from the book she was studying in the Whistle Stop, Minnesota, library to see a tall, slim, muscled man sitting across from her. His dark, wavy hair fell lightly over his face; dimples graced both cheeks when he smiled. Giving him a puzzled look, she answered, "And you would want to know… why?"

He shrugged and winked. "Just noticed you sitting here and thought I would welcome you to town. I don't recognize you."

"Is he bothering you?" An older lady joined them. Angel guessed her to be about sixty-five years old. She wore a plain black shift that hugged her slightly plump body. "Don't mind Matthew here. He was just leaving." She gave the man a pointed look. "I'm Mayme, the head librarian. We don't allow riffraff like him to bother our patrons."

Matthew laughed. "All right, Aunty Mayme. I have to be going anyway as the guests will want their afternoon tea."

Hearing Matthew mention tea, Angel crooked her head to study the man. "You serve tea?" Her tone indicated her disbelief.

"He does. He owns the Brick Schoolhouse Bed-and-Breakfast next to my house. This is my nephew Matthew Harkin."

Matthew said, "Call me Matt. Aunt Mayme only calls me Matthew when I get in trouble or when she introduces me to someone. She thinks it's more professional for an owner of a B&B."

"You help your wife run a bed-and-breakfast? I heard there was one in town," Angel said.

Mayme burst into laughter.

Matt sighed and answered, "I don't have a wife. I run the Brick Schoolhouse by myself."

"No woman would want him. He's too particular. His mother stays with me when she comes to visit. She has to be too neat at his house," Mayme said, winking at Angel so she would know Mayme was teasing her nephew.

"I've got a room or two available if you need one while you are here," Matt said, his eyes twinkling with mischief.

Angel closed the book she was reading on the history of Whistle Stop. She stood and said, "No, I already have a place to stay, and I must get going or I'll be late. It's interesting learning about the town that's going to be my new home. I didn't know it was named after the railroad and it was a main hub for the trains, hence the name Whistle Stop."

"Our little burg holds many secrets. Right now you are one of them. You wouldn't by chance be the person who is going to give my B&B competition?" Matt asked. "I heard someone bought the dilapidated Stevens' house."

"And if I am?" Angel answered.

"It's haunted and it needs a ton of work. Carpenters and plumbers alone will cost whoever buys that house a fortune," Mayme answered for her nephew.

"The house has been empty for years. Who knows what critters might inhabit the place? If you're the new owner, call me and I'll exterminate the creatures for you while you stand on the counter so they don't get you. Matthew the mouser at your service." Matt took a bow just as Mayme swatted his arm, a chuckle escaping her lips.

"Don't mind Matt. He takes after his father and has a wicked sense of humor. Are you the person who bought the house? I heard she was in her early thirties and from out of town."

Angel picked up her purse from the table. "I am and I think I'll be fine with the repairs. I'm not as delicate as I look." Turning to Matthew, she looked him straight in the eye. "You might be the innkeeper, but I'm the carpenter. Perhaps I can help *you* with repairs when your B&B falls into ruin. Have a great day." She turned, walked past the history section, turned at the end of the aisle, and disappeared from view.

Mayme turned to Matt. "Was that any way to greet a newcomer to the city?"

Still looking in the direction Angel had walked he said, "I think this town just got a lot more interesting. I'm glad you talked me into turning the schoolhouse into a bed-and-breakfast, and you know you love mom staying with you. I know you do it as a favor to me to keep her out of my hair."

"Remember who gets credit for letting you keep that thick head of hair when Harry Trent comes calling at my house. I swear that man doesn't know how to take no for an answer. Thanks for inviting him over for tea yesterday and getting him out of my house. Even Dipper doesn't like him." Mayme was referring to her parakeet. "She squawks up quite a noise. Maybe I should let her out of her cage when he's there and she will peck him out of my house."

Matt laughed. "He's scared of her you know, told me so himself. He said it reminded him of Tippi Hedren in the movie *The Birds*."

"If you're not around, I'll remember that. Now go back to the B&B so I can get some work done." She picked up the book Angel had been reading. "Angel checked this out but forgot it. I'll put it behind the shelf for when she comes back."

Matthew picked up the book. "No problem. I think I'll just swing by the old Stevens' house after tea and see if she's there. I'll give her a history lesson."

CHAPTER TWO

Angel held the keys to her new queendom in her trembling hands. She put the key into the lock of the disheveled Victorian Home. Signing the final papers at the real estate office gave Angel a thrill, even though the changes she was making in her life made her shiver with thoughts of the unknown. She was opening the door to her new home.

It was strange Jerilyn Travis, her agent, hadn't made it to the closing. Jacob Tesla, the owner of the agency, took care of the closing without Jerilyn. Angel had met Jerilyn earlier at the house for a final walk-through. The agent was still at the house when Angel left for the library to pass the time until she was to return to the real estate office for the closing. Jacob hadn't heard from Jerilyn, but he didn't seem concerned.

Testing the lock on the door, she turned the key and heard the click of the dead bolt unlock. Turning away from the door to look around the yard, her eyes settled on her travel trailer. It would serve as her home for the summer. The 1984 Airstream Excelle she had renovated to her style of living would keep her comfortable during the property's transformation. Before exploring the house, she decided she would move the trailer over to the garage.

The electrical hookups on the garage would do for the moment. Since the garage was an old carriage house, Angel chose to work on that first and move into it before winter when she planned to start renovations on the big Victorian house. First thing in the morning she would look for an electrician to make sure the wiring would handle her camper and have him check the wiring of the carriage house to make sure it could accommodate a living space.

Most women wouldn't take the chance of traveling alone with a trailer hitched to her pickup truck, but Angel wasn't afraid. Her dad taught her how to be self-sufficient, and she was used to doing things on her own.

Jessie Delaight wanted to accompany his daughter to Whistle Stop, but Angel talked him out of it. He was busy trying to wind down from selling his business, the Delaight Construction Company located in Chicago. She also felt she could settle in better on her own, doing her own renovation without her dad's interference. It wasn't that she didn't want his suggestions, but they were alike in that they both wanted their own way, and right now she didn't want the added stress of butting heads with her dad.

Angel backed the Airstream down the long driveway by the side of the house and parked on the grass next to the carriage house. That way she could put her truck in the garage and it would be out of the way during remodeling of the upstairs.

Old oak and apple trees surrounded the house and carriage house. A weed and random tree-covered path meandered through the back of the property to a little creek. Peppered throughout the grove were also pine trees. Angel suspected many of the trees grew on their own after the property had been abandoned.

There was a peacefulness surrounding the grounds and especially the woods. Perhaps she would put up a gazebo behind the large Victorian.

Patting the hood of her truck, Angel decided it was time to take her first steps as the owner into her newly purchased house. This was a far cry from Chicago and her loft apartment that overlooked Lake Michigan.

Could she become a country girl? She walked toward the door at the back of the house. It was time to branch out on her own after working as a carpenter and consultant for her father's business all these years. At thirty-five, she hadn't found anyone to share her life with, not even a cat or a dog. For some reason, in her mind, owning a pet in a loft apartment in the middle of a city wasn't much of a life for an animal.

Romance seemed to have escaped her too. It wasn't that she didn't have anyone interested in changing her single status, but at the last minute, right before she was to accept an engagement ring, she knew it wasn't for her. Every man she had met expected that after the vows were said, she would either quit working for her father as a carpenter —because it wasn't what women her age did—or they wanted her to change her career to suit his lifestyle.

Angel inspected the outside of the house before entering through the back door. *There certainly was a lot of work to do on this property.* She wasn't sure she was up to the challenge.

The panels covered the space where the large windows that surrounded three sides of the porch had been. With siding on the outside, passersby wouldn't have known the windows once existed. Replacing the windows would give the space a cozy feel, bringing in the sunshine to warm the room.

Whoever put the paneling over the windows forgot to seal the cracks, and there were spaces between the window and the wall as evidence they once existed.

Off the porch was a mudroom, or perhaps it had been a serving room. Although gutted, there were still signs someone had kept animals in the room. Remnants of water bowls and dried food still littered the floor.

Feeling sad at the neglect the old house had suffered, she moved on to the kitchen. Old white cabinets filled two walls. It was a big kitchen with a brick fireplace on one wall. An old cast-iron cookstove stood on another wall and next to it a seventies gas oven. The previous owners hadn't even removed the old stove. That was maybe a plus.

She took a peek into what had been the library. Thank goodness the oak woodwork was still in good shape. Bookshelves lined each wall with another fireplace on an inside wall. A large bay window opened to the back of the property.

Meandering through the dining room, she noticed it was in perfect condition. The walls were already restored, and the woodwork and built-in side cupboards had been refinished. Someone in the past started restoration in this room of the house, but who? Jerilyn had said it had been abandoned for years.

In the formal living room, piece of paneling had come loose from underneath the stairs. This was a change from when she did her earlier inspection and walk-through with Jerilyn.

Angel tapped on the wobbley board. Why anyone would install faux wood was beyond her, unless it was to cover the old plaster cracks. She decided to investigate the condition of the wall underneath, thinking the overlay was probably installed in the seventies. It seemed to have been the *in* thing back then.

Grabbing the side of the panel with her hand, she gave it a tug. It didn't give way immediately. Putting all her 110-pound body weight behind her, she used both hands and gave it another pull. It gave way and slammed against her, making her pitch backward. When she landed on the floor, a heavy weight fell on top of her.

Did part of the wall come down with the paneling?

Angel tried to move the section of wallboard off her. The weight of the large board and whatever was on it kept her pinned down and wouldn't budge.

Hearing a knock at the front door, she hollered, "Come in. I could use some help."

"I'm in. Where are you?" a voice said from the entryway.

"In the living room. It's forward and to your right," she answered.

"I brought— What happened?"

She saw feet from her position underneath the heavy weight holding her down. "There was a loose panel on the wall, and I pulled it down to see what shape the plaster walls were in, but it came down on top of me and I lost my balance. Part of the plaster must have come down too because there is something heavy weighing me down and I can't move."

"I… ah… don't know how to tell you this," Matthew Harkin said as he leaned down to examine whatever was on top of her. "But I think Jerilyn Travis pinned you to the floor. And she looks dead."

CHAPTER THREE

"You appear to check out fine, ma'am," the paramedic said as he finished examining Angel.

Angel stood up, brushed off her clothes, and ran a hand over her head, brushing her hair off her forehead. "Thank you. And what is your name?"

"My name is Tracy Ambruster."

"I'm Angel Delaight. I wish we could have met under other circumstances. Excuse me, I think the police officer needs to speak with me."

Angel walked over to where Matt and a uniformed officer stood discussing the body of Jerilyn Travis.

"Ted, this is Angel. I'm sorry. I didn't catch your last name," Matt said, introducing her to the officer.

"Delaight, Angel Delaight. I can't believe this is happening."

"I'm Ted Pangborn, Chief of Police of Whistle Stop. Our detective for the county will be here shortly, along with the medical examiner. Can you tell me what happened?"

Angel looked at the body of her realtor splayed out on her floor. The paramedics had rolled the five-foot-seven heavy woman off the paneling so they could rescue Angel. Wiping a tear from her eye, Angel turned her head from the scene to look at the chief.

"I saw a loose piece of paneling. It hadn't been loose when I did the walk-through of my house with Ms. Travis. I planned on pulling all this paneling off at some point to see if the plaster walls were damaged. I was curious what I was dealing with. I gave a yank and this panel fell on me. I thought it brought part of the wall with it until Mr. Harkin arrived."

"And Matt, why did you stop in? Ms. Delaight has barely set foot in town until today," asked the chief.

"We met at the library. She mentioned she was buying the house. To my good fortune, she forgot the book she checked out from the library. I told my aunt I would deliver it to her." Matt smiled at Angel. "It was a good excuse to see her again. When I got here, I found her under the sheet of wood and Jerilyn on top of the pile, not moving."

"You didn't move the body?" The chief turned and surveyed Jerilyn's still form.

"No, it concerned me Ms. Delaight was hurt and I might make it worse. I helped the paramedics lift Jerilyn off the paneling so they could reach Ms. Delaight and determine she didn't suffer any injuries."

"What happened to her?" Angel could see a tinge of blood around her realtor's throat.

"That is for the medical examiner to determine," Ted Pangborn answered. "Did you know about the hidden passageway to another room?"

Angel lifted her head to peer past the chief and looked at the gaping hole revealed when the paneling had fallen. "Really? No, but that is exciting."

"When was the last time you saw Ms. Travis?" the chief asked.

"She took me around for the walk-through and stayed behind to lock up. That was this morning," Angel answered.

The front door opened and a woman about Angel's age came in.

"What ya got for me, Chief?"

"Ms. Delaight, this is Lila Henshaw, medical examiner for the county."

Lila nodded at Angel before looking at Jerilyn's body on the floor. "They told me it was Jerilyn. What are you thinking, Ted? A heart attack? Doc Wooster warned her she was cruising for one if she didn't lose some weight and change her lifestyle. Nice lady."

"I suspect someone helped her leave this planet, what with the tinge of blood on her neck," Ted answered. "Manner of death is for you to decide. As for the rest of you bystanders, it's time to vacate the scene."

"I live here now," Angel reminded him.

"I see you have a travel trailer parked out back," Ted said.

"Yes. I plan on staying there until I get the carriage house renovated and then live there until I finish the house," Angel answered.

"I suggest you stick to the plan. In the meantime until we figure out this situation, the house is off-limits. I also will call one of my deputies to keep an eye on the house until we determine what happened. We don't want you to be in danger," Ted said.

"I thought I was moving to a small, charming, safe community, and now this happens. Is there something the realtor didn't tell me about this town? How high is the crime rate here? I should have checked it out."

Matt laughed. "It is practically nonexistent. The most that usually happens is the police get called for a noise complaint when someone's rooster is crowing too loudly, or old Jeb Hawkins needs a ride home from the bar."

"I should have asked that question before I fell in love with this house," Angel said.

"We'll protect you, pretty lady." A new voice interrupted their conversation.

Angel bristled at being called a pretty lady by a strange man she didn't know. "And you are?" she said in her haughtiest voice.

"Barney Pipe, at your service. I'm Ted's right-hand man—or policeman, that is. And I'm no relation to that dude from Mayberry.

My mother loved Andy and Barney, and since our last name was Pipe, she thought it would be fun to name me after Barney Fife."

Angel's face wiggled in confusion. "Who is Barney Fife? And by the way, I'm not your *pretty lady*."

The men laughed.

Matt said, "We're too young to remember. Look up *The Andy Griffith Show*, and you'll see that Barney here was aptly named. No offense, Barney."

"I didn't mean any offense calling you pretty lady, even though you are pretty. I'm here to protect you. Chief Pangborn called. I'm a policeman here in Whistle Stop. I get the night shift."

Lila Henshaw's team came in the front door.

"It's time to clear out and let my team work. I'm officially booting you all out. This could be a crime scene," Lila announced.

CHAPTER FOUR

Angel put her face in her hands and tried to stop shaking. Leaning back on her sofa in the Airstream, she was glad she'd kept it together in front of the law enforcement team and Matthew Harkin, but now she felt the shaking take over her body. Even though this wasn't the first dead body she had encountered in her business dealings, this was the first one they thought perhaps had a murder.

Back in Chicago, she'd encountered a dead body in a home Delaight Construction bought for renovation. It was a homeless person who died during the brutal cold winter. Instead of fear, finding someone who passed away because of their living circumstances made her feel sadness and helplessness because she knew it happened too often to count.

Jerilyn's death not only was unsettling because it might be a murder but because it was someone she knew, if only briefly, and it took place in the house she planned to call home.

It was almost dinnertime. The locals would call it supper, but she was still in Chicago mode. There were no groceries in the trailer. Angel had planned a trip to the grocery store after inspecting the house.

A knock interrupted her reverie.

"Yes?" she asked tentatively, knowing she might have to be careful about opening the door to strangers.

"It's me. Matt."

She got up from the couch to unlock the door. "Hi, Matthew. I was just about to make a trip to the grocery store. It's been quite an afternoon. Come in. I want to thank you for showing up just when you did. I might have lain there all night."

"I doubt that, and call me Matt." Stepping inside, he gave the trailer a quick inspection with a few turns of his head. "This is beautiful—unexpected for an older Airstream."

"I prefer to call you Matthew, and yes, I renovated it when I bought it. The Airstream was my second home when I was working for my father."

"You worked for your father? You said earlier you were a carpenter. What kind of business did he have?"

"He owned a large construction company in Chicago, and not only did we do the big high-rise condos, we also specialized in building smaller homes too, finally getting into tiny houses. We ran the gamut," Angel answered.

"And you were one of his nail pounders?"

Angel's look should have scared the hardiest of men. "It was my job to oversee the construction, and occasionally I got my hands dirty too. That was my favorite part of the job. I lived out of my trailer. I would park it on site and stay for months at a time."

"Would you like to come to the Brick Schoolhouse for dinner. I have to cook for my guests, and it has been quite a day for you. I thought you might be too tired to make yourself a meal."

Angel considered his offer. "I *am* exhausted, and the thought of a meal already made is tempting." Angel brushed a hair out of her eye.

"And our grocery store closes at six. That doesn't give you much time to shop for your groceries." Matthew's eyes twinkled.

His eyes twinkled in the library too. *Maybe she should call him twinkle eye.* Smiling at the thought, she answered, "Six o'clock at night? Your grocery store closes at six? How does that go over with your residents?"

Matthew laughed. "They are closed on Sunday too. We aren't Chicago, and Whistle Stop decided a long time ago they weren't going to follow the pack when it came to always being open. So is tempting a yes?"

"I suppose it is. Thank you."

He opened the door to leave. "It should be ready in about an hour."

"How do I find this place?" She pulled up her phone to put the location in her GPS.

"Go out your driveway and turn right. In five blocks, turn right again by the Lutheran church, continue past the cemetery, and then take a left at the first street. At the end of the block you will see the Brick Schoolhouse on the corner."

Angel's eyes were wide. "You don't have an address?"

Matthew's eyes twinkled in merriment.

Do his eyes ever stop twinkling?

"I could have told you to turn by the Dobbs' house, and then when you get to my aunt's house, I'm right next door, but you don't know the Dobbses yet."

"I guess I'll get used to the quirks of a small town."

"Before I leave, I'll tell the police you are coming to the B&B for dinner and will be home later. Until they decide what happened with Jerilyn, they'll know your whereabouts in case it isn't safe. Although, this is Whistle Stop and we don't even lock our doors, so I'm sure this is just a fluke."

"Nice to know." Angel shut the door behind him. "Nice to know. What did I get myself into?" At least she had quit shaking.

CHAPTER FIVE

———————

Angel nodded while lifting her soupspoon to her mouth and listened to the questions asked of her by the other guests. Being careful not to slurp, she put the warm liquid to her lips, taking a moment to savor the taste before answering the burly man at her right.

"I'm excited to move to Whistle Stop even though they found a deceased person in my new home."

Charlie Mattson took a moment to look around the table at the other guests who were sharing the meal at the Brick Schoolhouse Bed-and-Breakfast. Turning back to Angel he said, "I must tell you your house is the very reason I came to Whistle Stop, but you made an offer right before I got to town to view the property."

"What do you do, Mr. Mattson?" June Middlebury, another one of the guests, asked.

"I buy and sell properties. We go in and access a property, decide if it is worth salvaging, be it a home or a business, and then if we deem it worthy, we restore it or bring it up to code and resell it."

June picked at her plate before turning her attention to Angel. "It must have been scary finding a body in your house, especially your real estate agent."

"It wasn't quite the way I expected my first day on my new property to go." Angel decided it was time to change the subject. "What brings you here, Ms. Middlebury?"

"The Brick Schoolhouse. I love to travel the country and try out different bed-and-breakfasts and visit small communities. Then I write about it on my blog."

"Is that something you do on vacation?" Angel asked.

"No, I do it full time. I make enough money from my blog to handle some of my expenses. I happen to have been born with a silver spoon in my mouth, so to speak, so money is not an issue. Please, call me June."

Bridgette, a young high school girl that Matt employed part-time, cleared the soup and salad plates as Matt came in from the kitchen and began serving the main entrée.

"Do you do the cooking, Matthew?" Angel asked.

"I do. It was my hobby for many years, and once I opened the B&B, I finally got to put my talent to the test, although my aunt helps out too."

"You do know the house you bought is haunted?" Charlie asked, watching Angel's face carefully to see if the detail he just provided brought any sign of trepidation.

"I had heard that. I also was in the library this afternoon doing some research on my house and the town. That's where I met Matthew."

"And that's how I came to rescue Ms. Delaight from Jerilyn." Matt came back into the dining room with Angel's plate and set it in front of her.

"Rescue you from Jerilyn?" A frown creased June Middlebury's forehead. "Did she attack you?"

"The paneling attacked her, and Jerilyn's body was on top of the paneling," Matt explained.

"If finding the body and the possibility of a ghost haunting your new home bothers you, I would be happy to make you an offer on the house," Charlie said to Angel. "I don't pay attention to those types of mishaps and blather."

"Aren't you nervous staying there tonight after that happened?" June asked.

"She has protection, and they still haven't determined how Jerilyn died," Matt answered for Angel.

Angel said, "I don't scare easily. I grew up in Chicago."

"That explains it." June shook her head. "Chicago is tough, in some parts of it at least. What is it you do for a living, Angel?"

"I'm a carpenter. I used to work for my dad's construction company, and we seem to have something in common, Charlie. Not only did we specialize in commercial building and apartment complexes, we also wanted to give back to the community, so we did a little renovation to put some homeless families into affordable housing."

"A little tiny thing like you a carpenter?" Charlie guffawed. "You're pulling my leg."

"You wouldn't have a little bit of a chauvinistic attitude there would you, Charlie?" Angel turned to face him.

"No, no, ma'am. I didn't mean a thing by that." Charlie put up his hands in defeat, showing he meant no harm.

"Oh dear, there are red lights flashing outside your house, Uncle Matt," Bridgette said as she came back to clear the plates. "I hope they're not here for me." She went over to the window to peek out onto the street.

"And why would they be here for you, Bridgett?" Her uncle's voice held a tinge of sternness.

"I… maybe didn't come home last night?" Bridgett answered.

The doorbell rang.

"You stay right there. We will finish this conversation unless they are going to haul you away in cuffs to your parents' house," Matt ordered as he went to answer the door.

"Hello, is the little missy here?" Barney Pipe's voice rang out in the entryway as he came into the house.

"I guess I'll go and start the dishes," Bridgette said, hastily leaving the room.

"If you value your life, you won't call her the *little missy*, Barney," Matt warned the police officer.

"Aw shucks, you know I don't mean anything by that, Matt. I like the little lady," Barney answered.

"It's fine, Matt. Barney, if you want to find out what a little lady does and you keep calling her a little lady in that condescending tone, you might want to rethink that thought. What do you need me for?" Angel asked.

"You can go home. It's safe. We're done with the crime scene. Chief Pangborn and Lila said there's no need to worry. He's even pulling the patrol," Barney said to the group.

"It wasn't a homicide?" Angel asked.

"I can't answer that. He just said you can go back home and rest in peace. Wait, I don't mean the *rest in peace* as the funeral rest in peace, but where you can rest in peace because no one is going to make you into a dead person." Barney wiped his brow. "You keep confusing what I'm saying. I saw it on your face. I'm going home now. Two dead people in one day are too much for me."

"Two dead people?" The entire table blurted the words out at the same time.

CHAPTER SIX

Angel still didn't know what happened last night to clear up the crime scene at her new home. She gleaned the case must be closed because when she arrived back at her travel trailer after Barney Pipe's announcement that there were two dead people, there was no crime-scene tape left on the property and no police officer guarding her house. Matthew offered to see her home, but she insisted he stay with his guests. It was only a few blocks, and if the police said she was safe, she took them at her word.

It was a beautiful summer day. Angel decided it was time to get started on the carriage house, but first she was going to pay a visit to Chief Ted Pangborn and find out what happened to Jerilyn Travis and who the second dead body was. She surmised the murder investigation was over since Barney Pipe wasn't overly concerned about the case anymore. But before she did either of those things, she was going to the house to check out the room underneath the staircase that was revealed when she had pulled off the paneling and found Jerilyn.

Ready to turn the key to lock her door, she remembered she was in Whistle Stop, Minnesota. *Hadn't Matthew said they didn't lock doors here?*

She pocketed the key and walked down the driveway to the house, letting herself in the front door instead of the back.

All seemed quiet in the big Victorian. The paneling was no longer lying on the living room floor. In fact, it was nowhere to be seen. She walked over to the gaping space underneath the steps. It was a cute reading nook with a bookshelf on one side and a bench underneath the steps on the other. Since the steps going upstairs were wide, the room was the size of a foyer. The other side of the reading nook was open to another room. It was nicely built, making it almost one space.

Walking through the opening into the previously hidden room, she saw there were no windows. From the outside of the house there was nothing to indicate that the room existed.

She went back out into the living room and looked at the walls. The room was cleverly hidden. The steps were on one side and the library wall was on the other side. No one had noticed there was a discrepancy in the footage.

A tap on the door shook her out of her reverie. "Come in?" She probably should have first checked to see who was there.

"Ms. Delaight. I thought I would bring you up to speed on Jerilyn Travis." Ted Pangborn came into the room.

"I was just coming to see you, Chief Pangborn."

"Call me Ted."

"I heard last night there were two bodies. You didn't find both of them here? Or at least that's what I assumed since you took the crime-scene tape down and let me come back here without a policeman watching the property."

Ted Pangborn shook his head. "Tragic circumstances. Jerilyn was murdered by her brother. When we went to inform her husband, we found her car and her brother at her house. He was deceased. We speculate that he murdered Jerilyn, drove her car back to her home, and then took his life, distraught over what he had done to Jerilyn. It was a murder-suicide."

"That's awful. I forgot about this in the excitement of buying my new home, but I offered Jerilyn a ride back to the real estate office. She refused and said her brother was on his way to pick her up with her car. He apparently borrowed it that morning. How did she die? There was that small amount of blood around her neck."

"Dixon has had some issues of late." Chief Pagnborn seemed preoccupied with a spot on his shoe, leaning down to take a swipe at it before he continued. "He and Jerilyn were in a feud about the property her father left her. Jerilyn put it up for sale without his permission. That could be why their father only left it to Jerilyn."

"That seems unfair since they were both his heirs," Angel said.

"He maybe knew Dixon would not want to sell. Her father left instructions for it to be sold and to split the proceeds between the two of them. This was the property. Dixon claimed it was his legacy and he wanted to live here. We found this book open to this page with this paragraph highlighted."

Angel took the book and read the paragraph. *"The string of thread, sharp and precise, cut a line into his finger as the left hand pulled it tighter around the ring finger of his right hand. Tinges of red seeped onto the floor, dripping slowly and forming a small pattern of dots. Loosening the thread, the left hand pulled it away from the finger and let it fall to the ground. Raising his right-hand ring finger to his mouth, he kissed the finger before licking the blood away. Perfect, just perfect. His mind imagined a wire replacing the thread and a neck replacing the finger. Yes, it would be perfection."*

She handed the book back to Ted. "What does that have to do with Jerilyn's death?"

"He must have gotten the idea on how to murder his sister from this book, but then at the last minute he backed down. The bleeding from her neck came from a wire we think was wrapped around her neck, but it wasn't what caused her death. She actually died from a heart attack that Lila determined happened while Dixon tried to strangle her with the wire, so he didn't have to go through with it. Her weight has always been a problem, and Lila wasn't surprised that it's what killed her."

Angel sat down on the floor stunned. "That is quite a story. If I were a writer, it would make a perfect novel."

"Dixon must have known about the hidden room underneath the

stairs, and since he only weighed one hundred eighty pounds, he knew he couldn't get a two-hundred-fifty-pound woman out of there on his own without being noticed. At least that's what we figured."

"Is this just speculation, or did he leave a note explaining the details?" Angel asked.

"We've closed the case. He didn't leave a note, but it's obvious that's what happened. We had to track down Jerilyn's husband last night and give him the news. He was in Chicago on a business trip. It's quite a coincidence that you are from Chicago too, and Henderson Travis was in Chicago.

"Chicago is a big city, Chief."

"That it is. I best get going. I have to talk to Lila so I can complete the paperwork for the case. Just wanted you to know there was nothing more to worry about, and I'm sorry your first day was so traumatic. Welcome to Whistle Stop."

"I'll walk you out. I was checking out the house before I go downtown to see if I can scope out some breakfast, buy some groceries, and head on over to the hardware store for some supplies for the carriage house. I believe you have a lumberyard combined with a hardware store called Pick It Up?"

Ted held the door for Angel to precede him out. "We do. Tell Art Groenewald to treat you right, or he will answer to me."

"As long as he doesn't call me *little lady*, we will get along fine," Angel warned.

CHAPTER SEVEN

"Why don't you join me?" Lila Henshaw motioned to the other chair at her table at the White House Eatery.

"I would be happy to," Angel answered. "I'm impressed. When I looked at the outside of this restaurant, I wondered if I might want to come in. It's a little nondescript and old."

Lila smiled. "It's white, big, and bulky isn't it? Hence, the name, the White House, but it has good food and it's been here a long time. We tend to keep our old buildings in these small towns."

"I'm glad I ran into you. I have questions about last night."

"So do I," Lila answered. "But what do I know; I'm only the county medical examiner." She shook her head while sipping her hot coffee.

"Can I get you something to drink?" Bridgette, the same young high school girl who was a waitress at the Brick Schoolhouse Bed-and-Breakfast, put down a menu in front of her.

"You do get around. I thought after announcing you did not go home the night before, your parents would have locked you up, not to mention Matthew. He seemed overly upset at the news. I suppose it's because he is your uncle and one of your employers. Shouldn't you be in school?" Angel asked.

Lila answered for Bridgette. "It's Saturday and her parents will probably lock her up tonight."

"Lila, let's not give them any ideas. We haven't discussed it yet because they were called out on an ambulance and fire call before I got home," Bridgette informed them.

Angel looked closely at Bridgette. "Is your dad Tracy Ambruster?"

"Yes. I heard he was the one who checked you over when Jerilyn fell out of the wall," Bridgette answered.

"Her mother, Stacy, is Matthew's sister," Lila explained.

"Tracy and Stacy. I bet there are a few jokes about their names rhyming," Angel said. "I'll have some coffee, and you can add an egg and toast to that. But coffee first, please."

"I'll be right back with the black brew," Bridgette answered. "And I think my uncle is sweet on you."

"That was unexpected," Angel said after Bridgette left to put in their order.

"Don't take it personally. Bridgette has been trying to hook up her uncle for years, and you seem to be her new target."

"Let's talk about last night. I got a long explanation from Ted Pangborn this morning on how Jerilyn was murdered by her brother, and then he committed suicide at her home. It was a book that gave him the idea?"

Lila nodded. "That's the theory. We found a pill bottle by his body, and the toxicology reports indicated he died from an overdose and alcohol poisoning. Of course he didn't leave a suicide note, but the only fingerprints on the bottle were his and also were the only fingerprints on the book. Plus they found the wire that they conclude he had wrapped around Jerilyn's neck."

"It still seems strange. Why did he want my house so badly?" Angel asked.

"No one seems to know the why; we just knew he was very angry that she had sold the house, but she was just following the instructions her dad had left."

"Do you agree with the theory?" Angel asked.

"I do and don't, but this is Whistle Stop where things usually aren't too complicated. Jerilyn and Dixon were born and raised here and finally came back to live. They are one of Whistle Stop's own, so there is no reason to think anything else happened."

"Apparently it was no secret they weren't getting along," Angel said.

"Their feud was well known. Case closed, I guess, but that house has a history of strange things happening there, hence the rumor it is haunted. I read too many mystery novels. However, I also got my training in a bigger city, so I'm always suspicious, but there are no red flags here except my intuition. Maybe I'm just longing for the excitement of my old life," Lila explained.

"Why did you move here?"

"Why did you? I'm a fan of cozy mysteries. I know. Don't laugh. But it's true. Working where I did, I saw so many gruesome things I needed something to relax, and I got hooked on the idea of a cozy small Mayberry-type town. I was on my way to Omaha and took the back roads, wandered around, and drove through Whistle Stop, then fell in love with the old houses and the cute Main Street. I knew I had to come back here. When the job of medical examiner for the county opened up, I applied and here I am."

"I moved for the same reason and look what happened. I found a dead body."

Bridgette came back with Angel's coffee. "And my uncle rescued you. Shouldn't you ask him over for dinner tonight since he fed you last night? Whoops, don't answer that yet. I have to get your food; it's ready."

"I think you have a real cupid there," Angel remarked. "Why would she stay out all night?"

"It's not what you think," Lila explained. "Bridgette and a couple of her friends have formed a rescue group. They go out at night and rescue feral animals such as cats and dogs. The animals roam more at night, and some are in dire shape as they don't always get enough food, or people leave them on the country roads to fend for themselves. Her group goes out in the evening to rescue the animals, but at times they get so engrossed in what they are doing they forget about the time. Even in Mayberry there are dangers, so they are to be home by at least eleven. There are drugs in the county, and their parents don't want them to run into any of the underground activities that take place in the night."

"Drugs are big here too?" Angel shook her head. "I guess nowhere is safe."

"People don't like to talk about it, and while it doesn't disrupt our way of life here, it's a problem that no one talks about. You will find unsafe things happen occasionally in a small town, but all in all this is a great place to live. It really is Mayberry with a little Barney Pipe thrown in."

Bridgette came back and set Angel's food in front of her and then was about to pour Lila another cup of coffee when Lila said, "This is my last cup." Lila put her hand over the cup. "I better get over to the Police Station and meet up with Ted. He's expecting my final report. Watch out for this one or there will be a Rover in your future."

Bridgett frowned. "No, not a Rover, but I have a Garfield for you."

CHAPTER EIGHT

After stopping at the hardware store for cleaning supplies, Angel popped into the library for a few minutes to talk to Mayme.

"You have had an exciting time since I saw you last," Mayme said when Angel came in the door. "If you're here for the book you left, I gave it to Matt to give to you. Did he forget?"

"No, and I'm very happy he delivered it to me because he delivered me out from under Jerilyn too. My small body has a lot of muscle, but I couldn't wrestle that big piece of paneling along with Jerilyn's body off me. I think I was stunned for a few minutes after the paneling hit me."

"I'm happy you suffered no ill effects except for the trauma of Jerilyn's death. She was a nice woman. What brings you back to the library?"

"I thought I would ask you if you knew of anyone I could hire to help me with the house. I could have asked the man at the hardware store or Matthew, but somehow I felt your opinion would be honest and unbiased."

Mayme laughed. "That it would. What about Jerilyn's husband, Henderson? He may need something to keep him occupied now that Jerilyn's no longer here."

"I know he was on a business trip in Chicago when Jerilyn was killed. She was in her late fifties. Is he the same age?"

Mayme nodded. "Somewhere around there, but Henderson is from the Travis-Brisbane family. I'm not sure what they dabble in, but he doesn't need to work, so he picks up handyman jobs once in a while just to keep busy. It's his hobby. He builds furniture and restores old pieces in his barn at the back of their property."

"I've heard of Travis-Brisbane. I didn't connect the two. They have offices all over the world. He's that Travis?"

"He is. He retired at fifty-five years old and turned the running of the company over to his son, Jerald Travis, named after his mother as you can tell. Again, I'm not sure what they do. Jerilyn and Henderson never like to talk about it. They just want to be one of the folks."

"I know what they do. They are big into real estate holdings, building and also buying large factories and hotels and office buildings for the elite," Angel answered. "I'll wait a few days and see if he is interested."

"Poor Henderson. He and Jerilyn were soul mates. I know she was heavy, and he is... well... what we would say in my day... a dish. But they were two peas in a pod. He will be devastated."

"I forgot to ask why Jerilyn's brother was at their house," Angel said.

"That's easy. He was living there. Formerly he had his own home over by the lake, but it burned down not too long ago, right around the time their father died, which could be why he was so desperate to keep the Stevens' house."

"That's another question I forgot to ask. If it belonged to Jerilyn or her father and Dixon's name is Warner, why is it called the Stevens' house?" Angel asked.

"According to the history of the town, Jerilyn and Dixon's grandfather and mother were both a Stevens, and the name has stuck all through the years because I think it was originally built by his great-grandfather," Mayme explained. But their father wasn't living in the Stevens' house. He had his own home over on the lake."

"Has Dixon ever been married?"

"Many years ago Dixon had a fiancée, and one day they had a spat. She left town. It was said she wanted a career in show business, and Dixon wanted to stay in Whistle Stop and run the family business, which he did. He ran it right into the ground. After that happened, he became a recluse."

"Isn't that hard to do in a small town? No one is letting me be a recluse."

Mayme handed Angel a stack of books. "You can help me put these away."

Angel took the books and followed Mayme.

"I believe the only person Dixon let into his life was a friend from his childhood and college. He did go to college and that was where he met his fiancée. The friend lived with him for a time, but when his house burned down his friend moved to Minneapolis." Mayme took a book off the pile Angel was holding and put it on the shelf before continuing her explanation. "Rumor has it Dixon was helping him out of a tough time and that he had been homeless. Dixon found him and took him in. He's probably homeless again unless he found a job. It wouldn't work to be homeless in Whistle Stop. There's nowhere to hide, and I'm sure we don't have any support in place to help homeless people. We just don't have homeless people in Whistle Stop; at least I don't think we do."

Angel handed Mayme the next book and said, "I would suspect there are homeless in all our communities no matter how small if we look for them."

Mayme stopped for a moment to consider Angel's statement. "If it was one of our own, I know this community would help them out in a minute. But strangers are a little harder for them to accept. Here I am running around at the mouth. Matt would be so upset with me. Thanks for helping." She took the last book from Angel's arms.

Angel laughed. "That's fine. It's good to get a little of the history of Whistle Stop so I don't run afoul of any... town rules. I must get going. I also need a plumber and electrician. Where might I go for that?"

"That I would ask Matt; he had the entire schoolhouse plumbed and rewired." Mayme gave Angel a sly smile.

Angel caught the look and said, "No matchmaking. Maybe I'll hire some crew from my father's former business. I just didn't want to tip off my father that I was hiring."

<h1 style="text-align:center">CHAPTER NINE</h1>

Angel decided to spend some time in the carriage house when she returned to her new property. She wasn't quite ready to tackle going back into the house where she'd found Jerilyn's body, although she was intrigued by the new room that was discovered. It would make a nice reading nook and office. *What else they would uncover when the walls were pulled down?* A tinge of excitement filled her veins at the thought, before sadness set in thinking of how Jerilyn's life ended. Jerilyn was someone she had hoped she would be friends with when she moved to Whistle Stop.

After setting her cleaning supplies down in the lower portion of the carriage house, she decided to sketch out the changes she wanted to make, starting with the upstairs, which was going to become her apartment.

The railing on the stairs wobbled as she held on to it. It was going to have to be fixed right away and the stairs repaired so they were strong and steady for carrying materials up to the second floor. She stopped and pondered whether to replace the steps completely with a wider girth, making them a showstopper on the side of the downstairs room.

When she reached the second floor, Angel surveyed the room

before looking up at the ceiling. She imagined skylights overhead letting the sun stream in, making it the perfect artists abode.

There were large french doors on the west side of the loft-like space. A wall separated the kitchen from the rest of the area. It would have to come down.

A tapping came from the downstairs front door. She heard it open. "Hello, Ms. Delaight, are you here?"

She didn't recognize the voice, but this was Whistle Stop and they knew her name, so how dangerous would it be to answer? "I'm up here." She wouldn't have done that in Chicago, but then the door downstairs would have been locked. She always locked her door in Chicago.

Heavy footsteps sounded on the stairs, and soon she saw the top of a head, red with a crew cut, make its appearance. She didn't recognize the man. He looked to be in his middle fifties, burly, not overweight but solid, about five eight once he actually stepped off the stairs. She couldn't help admiring how handsome he was.

"Can I help you?" she asked.

"I'm Henderson Travis." He offered his hand for a handshake.

Angel placed her hand in his firm grip. "I'm so sorry for your loss."

He dropped his hand from hers. "Thank you. I understand you are the one who found Jeri. I had to talk to you. I also understand you are probably the last person to talk to her when you had your walk-through."

She nodded. "I guess you're right. I hadn't thought about that. What can I tell you?"

"Did she seem upset or nervous or worried about anything?"

"No, she seemed normal. This was the third or fourth time I met her, but I talked to her on the telephone more because she found me this house and was handling the sale. I left her here. She said she was going to lock up and would see me at the real estate office," Angel answered.

Henderson wiped some wetness from his eyes. "I can't believe this happened all because she was going to sell this house."

"I know this is none of my business, but did you ever suspect her brother might murder her?"

He shook his head. "No, and I still can't believe Dixon would do that or take his own life. That just wasn't Dixon. He was always so happy-go-lucky, but he did get very agitated and upset with Jeri. He really wanted that house, but Jeri thought it would be best if it was finally out of the family. It held bad memories for both of them."

"Was that why the property had been left to ruin?" Angel asked.

"Yes. Jeri had a secret love for this place. Her mother grew up here and died here. Her mother convinced her family it held nothing but bad karma. Jeri didn't spend much time here with her grandparents out of respect to her mother. After her father died, it was still his. He'd inherited it when his wife died, and he left firm instructions that Jeri sell it. She agreed and thought if someone outside the family had it, the light would come back to this property."

"I've heard that people believed it was haunted. Did Jerilyn?"

Henderson laughed. "No, my sweet Jeri didn't believe in ghosts; she just believed in bad memories and thought if Dixon moved in here, his mood would change once he got close to the memories again. But still, as angry as Dixon was, he loved his sister. He would never hurt her, and I don't think he would hurt himself, but I have no explanation for any of it except the police at first thought I might have wanted them both dead."

Angel looked directly into Henderson Travis's face. She saw a man who was struggling to keep it together. She believed him. "I understand you do some handyman carpentry work."

Startled at the question and the change in the conversation, it took him a minute to answer. "I do that as a hobby."

"Well, I'm a carpenter and I know what I'm doing, but I could use a little help to get this carriage house into proper living conditions so I can live here while I finish the house. You were recommended to me by a friend. Are you interested?"

He looked around the big room. "I might be."

"You don't have to decide now. Wait until after Jerilyn and Dixon's funeral and then let me know. Do you have any other family?"

Henderson shook his head. "No, I was an only child, and Dixon was Jeri's only brother. My son Jerald will be coming for the funeral. My parents are dead."

"I'm sorry to hear that," Angel said.

"I better get going. I've taken enough of your time. Would you mind if I visited the house to see where Jeri died? I need some sort of closure, and I thought talking to you and seeing where she died might help."

Angel reached in her pocket. "Here's the key. Leave it on the fireplace mantel when you leave and don't lock up. I'm going over there later."

"You trust me to do that after the police thought I might have had something to do with my wife's murder?" Henderson looked her straight in the eyes.

"Henderson Travis, for some reason I do trust you. And I can't explain why, after living in Chicago all these years, trust doesn't come easily for me with strangers."

Henderson looked down at the keys in his hands. "Thank you. I guess you've found yourself a handyman too. I've thought it over, and I'll sign on for the long haul because you believe me." He gave a quick glance around the upper floor of the carriage house. "This is going to be a long haul."

CHAPTER TEN

Angel was finally taking a good look at the main house on her property. The crime-scene tape had been taken down. Henderson Travis had left. She had watched from the window of the carriage house as he drove away. She picked up the key on the fireplace and took a few steps into the space underneath the stairs, delighted with this discovery, even though it was Jerilyn who had seemed to discover it.

Pocketing the key, she walked around the staircase and inspected the woodwork on the steps. It could be restored easily. She wiggled the loose railing. The steps were sturdy with no creaks or soft wood. That was a good sign.

At the top of the stairs, she looked down the hallway. Maybe they could open it up so it overlooked the main room downstairs.

There were five bedrooms on the second floor. At the end of the hallway, tucked away, was another staircase into the attic. After inspecting each room, she made her way up to the third-floor attic. This was the floor that made her fall in love with the house. She could imagine it finished with a big window or skylight. It would be the perfect place to dream, write, and create.

Angel always dreamed of becoming an artist. She wasn't one to try painting anything but a wall, but now being in her new "discover me" mode, she might try it.

She heard a voice in the distance. Was someone really yelling "Girly, are you there?"

Making her way back to the second floor, she called out, "Who are you looking for?"

"You," the voice answered.

"Do you mean Angel Delaight?"

"Yes, girly, you."

"I'm not a girly. How many times do I have to tell you?" Angel said to Barney Pipe as she stomped down the steps to the first floor, steaming at being called girly again.

"I'm sorry, missy. I don't mean any harm. It's my way of being friendly but… um… I don't mean in that way, I mean friendly like in I would like to be your friend," Barney answered.

Angel looked at the policeman and decided to give him a break. "Barney, if you quit calling me girly, we can be friends. Is that a deal?"

Barney held his lips together in thought. "I'll… uh… try."

"What can I do for you, Barney?"

"I heard that you need a little hammering and nailing, and I come to offer my help."

Angel gave the policeman a confused look. "You're a policeman."

"Yah, but I like to pick up a hammer once in a while. See this hand." Barney held it out for Angel to see.

"It's black and blue."

"I got that trying to hammer my footstool back together. I just wanted you to know that I'm a jack-of-all-trades."

Angel eyed his hand. "I see. I'm not hiring right now. I just hired someone."

"No… no… you've got it wrong. I don't want you to hire me. I'm volunteering. You could look at it this way. I work for free and you put in a good word for me with Lila. I saw you having breakfast at the White House Eatery."

Angel slowly nodded. "I see. Hmm, I will ah… take that into consideration, but I really just met Lila."

"Just let me know when you need some help. Hang a hammer on your mailbox at the street and I'll know you need help. My last name isn't Pipe for nothing. Pipe up and I will pipe over."

Barney left as quickly as he came and before Angel could answer him.

Angel pulled her cell phone out of her pocket to check the time. Another knock on the door interrupted her.

"Angel, are you here?"

Angel decided the next time she was going to come to the main house she would lock the door behind her. She hadn't had this many visitors in one day while living in Chicago for as long as she could remember. In fact, she could go weeks on end at her apartment without talking to anyone in her building.

"Yes, I'm here." At least this time she recognized the voice.

"I heard you had a busy day, so I thought you might like to come back to the Brick Schoolhouse for another dinner." Matthew Harkin stood in the foyer of the house, not coming in any farther.

"And you heard I had a busy day how?" Angel questioned.

"I understand you had breakfast with Lila, then went to the hardware store, then talked to Aunt Mayme, and I saw Barney leaving here. He's quite the character, don't you think? Was there more news on the case?"

"You forgot Henderson Travis visiting. Your spies are falling down on their job."

Matthew laughed. "I missed a visitor? You need to get used to this. You now live in a small town and your neighbors know what you are doing before you do."

"If that's the case, why hasn't anyone figured out what happened to Jerilyn?"

"Good point. You'll have to ask Ted Pangborn about that, but last I heard he was closing the case. Now about dinner."

"I appreciate the invite, but I think I'll pass. I just want to settle in my trailer with a good book, a glass of wine, and have an early night. I didn't sleep very well last night thinking about Jerilyn."

A tap at the door interrupted them. Both Matthew and Angel shrugged their shoulders at the sound.

"Yes?" Angel answered tentatively, resigned to the fact that people in the community liked to drop in unexpectedly.

"I'm back!" Barney Pipe's voice preceded him into the room.

Angel saw something wiggling in Barney's arms. "Barney, I haven't made up my mind about your helping me yet."

"I brought you a housewarming gift. I forgot to bring her the last time I was here."

Angel frowned while Matthew smirked.

"Barney, that's a puppy. A big puppy," Angel said.

"Yup, yeserie, it's a labradoodle. I saved her from the shelter. They haven't found a home for her, and I knew she was just the guard dog for you." Barney set the puppy on the floor. The puppy immediately relieved herself.

Angel remained silent as she watched the puddle pool on the linoleum that she suspected covered a hardwood floor. She raised her eyebrows and her eyes narrowed into tiny slits when she looked at Barney.

"She's just excited. See, it's her way of saying she likes this home," Barney said.

"Barney, I don't know that Angel knows what to do with a dog." Matthew bent over to pet the black labradoodle.

"I've never had a dog, and I don't think I want one now," Angel said.

Barney took a buzzing radio out of his pocket. "Oops, got to go. Zebb's sheep are out on the road again. You can keep the Missy Four Foot; isn't that a great name? I dubbed her that when I picked her up. You can keep her while you are thinking about letting me help you. I put her things on the lawn. I have to go before those sheep get into old Mrs. Burnbaum's flowers. She'll have me planting new ones if I don't get them back home. See ya." Barney sprinted through the foyer and out the front door before Angel could protest.

Matthew cleared his throat and began to back up into the foyer. "I have to cook dinner. So sorry you can't join us." He turned and exited through the foyer before Angel could stop him.

Looking down at the labradoodle, Angel said, "I don't know what to do with you. But I guess you'll have to stay for a while, at least until I can get Barney to come and get you."

The labradoodle looked up at Angel, whined, and piddled on the floor again.

CHAPTER ELEVEN

The Lutheran church in Whistle Stop was almost full when Angel stepped inside. She slid into an empty seat next to the aisle in the back of the church. It didn't surprise her that so many people from the small community turned out for the funeral of Jerilyn and her brother. What did surprise her was the dual funeral. She didn't think if the same thing happened in her family, her spouse—who didn't exist yet but if she did have one—wouldn't be so magnanimous as to let her share her funeral with the brother who murdered her. But then she remembered that Henderson wasn't sure Dixon would have murdered his sister.

The only people she knew in the church were Matthew and his Aunt Mayme, Lila Henshaw, Tracy Ambruster, and of course, Henderson Travis. She didn't see Chief Ted Pangborn or Barney Pipe. Maybe it wasn't proper for the police to show up at a funeral even if it was a small town.

The music stopped, and a man stepped into the middle of the aisle. Since he had on a clergy collar, Angel surmised it was the pastor. He gave his welcome, and then the music started again and the family proceeded behind the pastor through the church to the front pews. It was a small procession.

Henderson Travis had a young man in his late thirties by his side. Angel assumed that was his son, Jerald. Following them were various men, women, and children who Angel also assumed must be related in some way or were friends since Henderson mentioned he didn't have any family left.

When the family was seated, the pastor began the service. Just after the sermon, Angel saw a movement out of the corner of her eye. Chief Pangborn had snuck into the church and slid into the pew on the opposite side of the aisle from her. She glanced at the chief. He saw the glance and nodded.

Angel turned her attention back to the front of the church. Barney Pipe took a place by the piano, and Bridgette, sitting at the piano, started to play. Bridgette seemed to be one with many talents, but what was Barney doing up front?

Angel watched as Barney opened his mouth. The words to the song "The Old Rugged Cross" seemed to flow out of his mouth. Barney was scrawny; at least Angel thought so, but his tone while singing was deep and rich. It seemed Barney Pipe was a man of surprising talents too.

Barney finished the song, looked out into the church, and said, "Mighty happy to do this for you, Henderson. Jerilyn was a peach pie." He looked embarrassed and quickly sat down in the front pew.

The pastor cleared his throat. "Yes, ahem, on that note, before we say our last goodbye to Jerilyn and Dixon, I want to remind you that there is lunch in the basement after the service, and we are serving Jerilyn's favorite pie, peach." The pastor winked at Barney. "You got that right, Barney. Jerilyn was a peach."

The pastor gave the final blessing, and Angel watched as Henderson carried Jerilyn's ashes out of the church. His son, Jerald, carried Dixon's. The rest of the funeral party followed them.

While they were waiting for the ushers to dismiss them, Angel whispered to the man next to her, "Will they bury them first before the meal or afterward? What is the proper procedure for this?"

The man leaned over and said, "I have no idea. I knew Dixon and just came into town for the funeral. He was a good man."

That was the first time anyone seemed concerned about Dixon, so Angel turned to get a good look at the man next to her. He appeared to be in his early fifties. His manner of dress suggested he might be a businessman, although his pants seemed a little too big for his bony body and his shirt had a lot of room to fill. But then it was hard to tell since his suit jacket appeared to be too small and maybe that was why the shirt appeared too big.

"Were you a business associate of Dixon's? I'm not sure what he did for a living."

"You might say that. And you are?" The man studied her face in detail.

Uncomfortable with the stare, she answered, "I'm new to town. I bought the Stevens' house. Oh, the usher is almost here. We're next." Angel stood up so she could end the conversation, and as soon as the usher reached the pew, she sped down the aisle and followed the others to the basement of the church.

"You look like you are running away. Not from me, I hope?" Matt Harkin stepped into line with her.

"No, although maybe I should be since you left me with the piddler last night," Angel answered.

Matt laughed. "I thought it was a good idea. I think she will grow into a good watchdog, and you are staying, right? So you have plenty of room for her. Why were you moving so fast?"

"I was a little uncomfortable with the man sitting next to me in church. He said he knew Dixon and Dixon was a good man and wouldn't murder Jerilyn. Then he gave me a look up and down that made me uncomfortable. So I left him in the dust."

Matthew handed Angel a plate from the food buffet. "It's not *sit-down* here; it's a serve yourself, but the food is fantastic because Mayme made it."

Angel took the plate and went down the line, filling it with food. She made sure she took a piece of German chocolate cake. Glancing around the room, she saw the man who had been next to her over by the door talking to Chief Pangborn.

"What, you didn't take any Jell-O? Haven't you heard that's a Lutheran specialty?" Matt teased.

She ignored the question and nodded toward the door. "That's the man. Do you know who he is?"

Matt looked in the direction she indicated. "I don't, but maybe you can get the chief to tell you or perhaps Barney. He seems smitten with you."

"He's smitten with Lila, and he seems to think since I had one breakfast with her, I'm the way to her heart for him." Angel said.

"I wonder if Henderson will stay in town now. I think the only reason he settled here when he retired was because of Jerilyn. She loved this town, and she loved her real estate career. It was something that was all hers. In the big city she was just the wife of a multimillionaire businessman—the trinket on his arm," Matt said.

"Is that the way Henderson felt or treated her?" Angel asked as she sat down at a table where three spots were still left open in the dining hall.

"No, he treated Jerilyn as if she walked on water." Matt picked up the coffeepot. "Would you like some coffee?"

Angel held out her cup. "This funeral is certainly different from the ones I've attended in Chicago. It's more personal and maybe more relaxed but in a good way."

"We have the best. Brass-Hintner Funeral Home takes care of everything. They take care of all the family's needs down to the meal, line up pallbearers, make phone calls, and see that there is a headstone eventually if the family wants one. They know the families, so it is important to them to make things easier during their time of loss."

"Very different from Chicago or Los Angeles for that matter. I attended a funeral of a relative. We got out of our cars, and they asked who wanted to carry the casket into the church. Nothing was arranged and the family wasn't even asked what hymns they wanted for the funeral. Speaking of hymns, I was very surprised at Barney Pipe. He has a beautiful voice and unexpected for a man of his size."

"He is full of surprises," Ted Pangborn said as he sat down in the only unoccupied chair at the table. "Have you met the others who are gracing your table?"

"No, they've been making googly-eyes at each other," a heavyset woman teased.

"Myra, leave the poor girl alone. She's new to town." The man at her side nudged the woman. "I'm Lester Scrat and this is my wife Myra. She means no harm, but she is an inveterate matchmaker, and she thinks Matt needs a match."

"No, she just thinks Matt should have a wife to run his bed-and-breakfast so he can get a respectable man job," the other man at the table said.

The man had a belly and a white beard like Santa, but Angel thought his attitude was more like someone whom Santa would have left coal for on Christmas morning.

"Meet Roger Madigan. He runs the Elevator in town. He's never been married because he can't find a woman who meets his expectations." Sheriff Pangborn winked at Angel.

"Fair enough Pangborn, fair enough. You know I was just joshing you, Matt. Your mother, whom I met last time she came to Whistle Stop, would have my hide if she thought I was serious. She's very proud of you. No offense."

"No offense taken, Roger." Matt turned his attention to Ted Pangborn. "Who was the man you were talking to over in the doorway?"

"That was the guy I've been trying to find. He's the homeless man who lived with Dixon before his house burned down. He introduced himself to me. I'm going to meet him later for questioning, but he made no bones of the matter that he thinks I've got it wrong and closed the investigation into Jerilyn's death way too early. He said Dixon wouldn't have touched a hair on Jerilyn's head and... he wouldn't have killed himself. The case is closed. There is just no evidence to the contrary. But I've wanted to talk to him, but I didn't know where the homeless man was. I'll see what he has to say."

Bridgette came over to their table and said to Angel, "Thanks for taking in the cute labradoodle. That was a nice thing for you to do.

Barney said you were delighted to get her. I'm so excited that you took her. Our shelter is getting overloaded right now."

Matt covered his mouth to stop the laughter that was bubbling and trying to spill out of his mouth. Angel gave him a dirty look.

"Actually I was hoping…" Angel started to address Bridgette.

"Oops, I have to go. I see someone who might take an animal." She left before Angel could finish her sentence.

"Well, girly." Roger Madigan chuckled. "I guess you will fit in this community like a mouse fits into a mousetrap."

CHAPTER TWELVE

Angel had left the black labradoodle locked up in the carriage house after checking to make sure no harm would come to the dog from any chemicals or anything the former owners left behind. She made sure she had a comfy bed and left a large bucket filled with water so the frisky puppy wouldn't get thirsty. The puppy liked to explore, and leaving her in the travel trailer with her excellent nose might have spelled disaster.

Opening the door to the carriage house, she expected the puppy to greet her, being tired of being locked up, but she was met with only silence. Looking over to the corner where she left the bed, she saw the animal was curled up and sleeping.

Angel saw a lump of black fur wiggle. The puppy was waking up.

She looked closer. The puppy wasn't waking up, but something was untangling itself from the little dog's fur. Two eyes peeked out at her. Whatever it was had black fur identical to the dog.

Was it a mouse? Angel backed up. Then she heard a tiny sound. The sound woke the puppy up, and she bent her head down next to her body and began licking whatever animal it was that belonged to the tiny eyes.

The puppy saw Angel, wagged her tail and got up to give Angel snuffles at her legs. A black kitten followed the puppy.

"No, no, no! We don't want a kitten. How did you get in here?" Angel bent down to pick up the tiny creature.

Glancing around the carriage house, she saw no signs of any other animals.

As she opened the door, the labradoodle puppy snuck past her into the yard. She set the kitten down outside the door. The black kitten sat at her feet and meowed at her.

"Now what do I do? Barney had better get back here and pick both of you up."

The puppy bounded off to sniff at the flowers growing out of control by the house. The kitten just sat and looked up at her as if expecting her to pick it up.

"Fine, I'll hold you for a few seconds, but I don't know what to do with you. What do you eat? Do you eat mice?"

She saw Matthew's car drive up. He parked the car and rolled down his window.

"What's that you've got in your arms?"

"I came home and found this snuggled next to the piddler. You need to call Barney and tell him to come and get both of them."

"He would be crushed. That's his housewarming gift to you. You can't give her back."

"And this little creature?" Angel kept petting the kitten.

"Is there a reason you don't want either of them?" Matt asked through the car window.

"I've never had an animal. I don't know anything about caring for them."

"Ask Bridgette. She knows animals. The shelter is full. Why don't you foster them until homes can be found or room opens up in the shelter?"

"Is there a reason we are talking through the car window?" Angel asked. "And what does foster mean? I know what it means to foster a child, but I've never heard of fostering animals. They might have done that in Chicago but I guess I didn't pay attention. Animals weren't really in my radar except to *not* want one."

"I came to issue an invitation to dinner. If you foster, the shelter pays for the vet bills and the food," Matthew explained.

"I was just to dinner the other night. I'm not sure I can take being called little missy again."

"I have someone staying at the B&B you might like to meet. You can ask Bridgette about the foster program."

Angel looked at the bush where the labradoodle was doodling. "I'm not sure I should leave her alone again so soon."

"Ah, you're hooked. I can tell. Bring her along and the kitten too if you want, but cats are much easier to leave alone. You'll need to go back to the store and buy some litter if you are going to keep it in your trailer, but you can also leave it to be an outside cat, but don't be surprised if it disappears and you never see it again. Who knows what critters hide in your woods and come out at night?"

"They would kill this cute little doll?" Angel gasped.

Matt nodded his head. "Yup, you're hooked. You can find litter at the grocery store and you might want to take it to the vet and make sure it doesn't have worms."

"Worms! Cats have worms?" Angel's eyes grew wide.

Matt stuck his hands through the window. "Give it to me. I'll drop it off at the vet and have it checked over, and you can pick it up when you come over for dinner."

Angel, thinking about worms, practically threw the kitten into his hands.

"It's fine, Angel. I'll get you a book about the care and keeping of cats. In fact, Bridgette probably has one."

"I guess I'll see you at dinner." Angel tapped the side of the car.

"Until we meet again." Matt secured the kitten in his lap before closing the window and driving away.

Angel noticed the puppy was chewing on something pink in the flower bed. She called to him, "Puppy, come here."

The puppy, wanting some attention, dragged whatever was in his mouth over to her.

"What do you have?" Angel took the object away from her. "It's a pink teddy bear. It looks recent. I wonder how that got here." Angel gave the teddy bear back to the puppy. I guess it's yours now. Should we call you Blink? Black plus Pink—Blink."

CHAPTER THIRTEEN

"You can leave your puppy out here to play with my dog." Matt showed Angel the fenced-in backyard of the Brick Schoolhouse.

Angel saw the black dachshund that was coming to meet them at the gate. "What is it with this town and black animals?"

"I got ole Angus from the shelter. Black animals are the last color to be adopted. So when I saw Black Angus, not the cattle type, I knew he was for me."

Angel wrinkled her nose in confusion. "Black Angus? Cattle?"

Matt laughed. "That's an instruction in country life I'll save for another time." He opened the gate, and the black labradoodle ran in to meet Matt's dog.

"Do you think they will be fine? They won't fight?"

"Angus is a lover. See." Matt pointed to the dogs already nudging each other and beginning to play.

"Blink, you behave yourself," Angel called to the dog.

"Blink?" Matt asked.

"Well, she found a pink teddy bear in the flowers and she looked good with the pink so black and pink is blink."

"I take it you are keeping her then. No need to call Barney."

"I suppose. Who am I meeting?" Angel asked as he led the way to the house.

He opened the door for her. "You'll see. The guests are all in the dining room, waiting for us."

The first person she saw when she entered the room was a tall, well-built man with dark hair that was thinning on top. The man's face crinkled into a huge smile. "Dad, what are you doing here?" Angel asked.

Jessie Delaight got up from the table and hugged his daughter. "This retirement stuff is a little boring, so I thought I would come to Minnesota and see your new home. I decided to stay here because, no offense, your Airstream isn't big enough for the two of us." He held out a chair at the table next to him for his daughter.

"You couldn't have told me?" Angel asked, partly annoyed that he surprised her. She had hoped he wouldn't visit until she had her renovations well under way.

Knowing what she was thinking, Jessie said, "I won't interfere unless asked, and I thought you might be able to use a little more muscle. I promise advice only when asked."

"Little missy, are you sure you don't want to sell that dilapidated place to me?" Charlie Mattson asked.

"I'm surprised you are still here, Mr. Mattson. Are you still looking for property in the area?" Angel asked and then added, "I'm not a little missy."

"That's right. I forgot. It's an entirely new time. It's hard to teach us old dogs new tricks," Charlie answered.

"What?" Angel was confused by his answer.

Her father laughed. "Charlie, my daughter's an independent woman and a city girl. She doesn't understand us old men and how hard it is for us to know the right thing to say anymore. But I'll tell you this; I wouldn't cross her."

"My, you folks are much too serious." Mayme brought in their salads. "Your father is a welcome addition to this B&B, Angel. He can stay as long as he wants."

Matt gave his aunt a speculative look before adding, "He certainly can, as can any of you."

"Why thank you. I'm sorry I'm only staying the night." A petite woman in her twenties who was fascinated by the earlier conversation spoke up. "How lucky you are that your father is interested in what you are doing. Mine just puts up the money so I don't bother him. May I ask what you are doing that he came to help you?"

Angel answered, "I decided to get out of the big city, and I fell in love with a Victorian house here in Whistle Stop. Since I'm a contractor and a carpenter, I decided to buy it, move here and fix it up, and live in it."

"She neglected to tell you she found a dead body in the house." Bridgett brought in their main dish. "Mayme checked on the dogs and they are doing fine."

"A dead body?" the woman screeched.

"You must have decided to keep the labradoodle," Bridgette continued.

"A dead body?" The woman wasn't giving up.

"Yes, I named him Blink." Angel still ignored the woman's question.

"A dead body? No one told me that." Jessie Delaight joined the conversation. "In your house?"

"Her real estate agent," Bridgette stated.

"We'll explain later. Why don't you eat this delicious food and talk about something more pleasant? Bridgette, doesn't Mayme need your help?" Matt took Bridgette's arm and led him out of the room.

"Are we in danger in this town?" The petite woman asked.

"No, it was a family matter and it's all over now," Angel answered. "Dad, I need to hire an electrician and plumber. Are any of our former electricians and plumbers available? I would be happy to foot the cost, knowing I have reliable people doing the job."

"They stayed on with the company when I sold it," her father answered. "We were fortunate to have our own tradesman. I could talk to the Williams brothers who bought the company and see if we could hire them in Minnesota. I'm not sure they are licensed to work here.

"I can help out there." Matt came back in with the dessert. "Their names are Jim and Jack Stanton. They are brothers, not quite twins, but they could be mistaken for twins. One is an electrician and one is a plumber. I can give you their number."

"Thank you." Angel took a bite of the dessert. "This is heavenly. I love cheesecake, and this melts in your mouth.

"It's Mayme's special creation," Matt said.

"And it's all I can do to have some of it left for dinner because this scalawag always tries to pilfer it before I can serve it." Mayme entered the room. "I hear you hired Henderson to help you with your project too. It'll be good for him and get his mind off Jerilyn."

"Mayme, you've lived here all your life. Are there any other relatives of the Stevens family living in this community? I would love to find them and ask if their relatives left any pictures or recollections of the house," Angel asked.

"Not that I know of, but I'll ask around," Mayme answered.

"Although you are excellent company, I think I'll retire to my room. All this talk about a dead body made me a little nervous. I think I'm happy to leave tomorrow. Hopefully I'll get out of this town alive." The petite woman got up from the table, nodded at them, and left.

"The newspaper tomorrow will dispel anyone's fears," Matthew said. "We have a weekly newspaper, the *Old Whistle Stop Times*. I imagine Jerilyn's death will be the lead story."

Charlie Mattson stood up. "Well if you all will excuse me, I'm taking a walk to burn off some of this food and see if I find any other houses that might interest me. Money talks you know, and usually if I see something I want, I get it, all except for little missy's house here."

Angel glared at the man and was ready to correct him again when Charlie held up his hands and said, "I know. I apologize. Ms. Angel's house is what I mean." He turned and left the room, muttering about women's lib and never understanding it.

Angel's face held the glare for a few seconds before she began to laugh. "Maybe we can teach an old dog new tricks. Is that the way you say it?"

55

CHAPTER FOURTEEN

It was a beautiful Minnesota evening when Angel got back to her trailer. She let the kitten outside and sat on a lawn chair to watch the stars in the clear night. She looked for the pink teddy bear to give to Blink. She had hidden it behind the potted geranium she bought earlier while at the hardware store. Blink hadn't wanted to leave without it, but Angel wasn't sure what would happen with Matthew's dog, so she hid it so Blink would leave.

Reaching behind the pot, her hand didn't come in contact with anything. She moved the pot. There was no pink teddy bear there. Maybe another animal had stolen it. Matthew had said there were raccoons in the area.

She called to Blink to come back to her and made him sit on her lap so she would be safe. The kitten had curled up underneath the lawn chair. Peering into the dark woods, she watched closely to see if she could see any beady eyes. After a few minutes, she relaxed and looked to the sky. The big dipper twinkled and seemed to be pouring water right on top of her.

Glancing toward the main house, she thought she saw a movement in the dark windows. Her forehead crinkled as she squinted and glared into the darkness. That was a movement, she was sure of it.

Reaching down to her cell phone that rested on her lap next to Blink, she picked it up and hit the emergency button.

Hearing the operator answer, she said, "I think there is someone in my house. This is Angel Delaight and I live at the old Stevens' house on... Oh, you know where that is. Thank you. Yes, I'll stay on the line. No, I don't see anyone right now. I'm not in the house but in the yard. No, I won't go into the house."

A siren interrupted her conversation with the operator. "Yes, they are here. Thank you." She hung up as the Whistle Stop police car pulled into the yard.

She stood up to meet the policeman.

"Stand back. Stay there. I'll check the house. Go into your trailer and lock the door." Barney Pipe was yelling across the yard at her. He was flashing something in his hand. "Is the door locked? If not, I'll break it down."

Angel shook her head in amazement. If someone was in the house, they certainly would know he was coming. "It should be locked. What if I brought you the key?" she suggested.

"No. No! I'll break it down. Get inside."

Angel decided it wasn't the time to argue. She picked up the little kitten and, with Blink already in her arms, carried them inside. She wondered if she should call Ted Pangborn, not being sure this was Barney's finest moment.

Letting the animals loose in her trailer, she kept the lights off as she looked out the window. She could see Barney was inside and shining the light from room to room. *Wouldn't it have been easier to turn the lights on?*

It seemed like hours before she saw all the lights come on in the house and Barney walking across the yard to the trailer, but in reality, it had only been ten minutes. Opening the door to her trailer, she stepped outside to meet him.

"Yes siree, it is dark out here. I think it was your imagination, little lady. Nope, no one there. And you're lucky; you *did* forget to lock the door, so I didn't have to use my muscle to break in. It's not a good thing forgetting to lock your door, especially after Jerilyn tipped the tulip. No siree." Barney wiped his forehead.

"Tipped the tulip?"

"Gave up the ghost or whatever you call it in the big city when someone bites the dust. Here in Whistle Stop we call it tipping the tulips."

"I know I saw someone, and I locked the door and… I'm not your little lady," Angel reminded him.

"I brought ya a present. Ya shouldn't leave things like this on the floor especially in an old house that isn't cleaned up yet. Germs you know. You might want to throw this in the washing machine. But I wouldn't use bleach to disinfect it from probable rat droppings. The bleach will fade the pink." He put the pink teddy bear that Angel had been looking for earlier into her hands.

She looked at the teddy bear and then at Barney. "This was in the house?"

"Yes siree it was. I was just joshing ya about the rat droppings. I didn't see any, but I would still disinfect it, although the floor seemed pretty clean where I found it. You must have done a little cleaning since ya been here."

Angel frowned. "Yes, well we had to clean up the blood from Jerilyn although there wasn't much."

"I didn't find the bear where Jerilyn died. I found it by the fireplace. Well toots, I have to go. False alarm, but make sure you lock the door. I flipped the dead bolt when I left, but I would put an extra lock on the handle. Awesome door by the way. Glad I didn't have to break it in."

Before Angel could say anything more, he headed down the driveway, hopped in his car, and drove away.

Angel held the bear in her hand and thoughtfully looked at the house. Maybe she did have ghosts. But ghosts who moved teddy bears?"

CHAPTER FIFTEEN

A loud pounding on Angel's trailer door woke her out of a deep sleep. She had spent the past few days finalizing her plans for the carriage house and ordering supplies from the local lumberyard. That, and always keeping a second eye on the main house at night to see if she spotted movement, had taken its toll when it came to sleep.

She looked at her phone by the bed. It was 6:00 a.m. Who was pounding on her door at six? Crawling out of bed, she stumbled to the door and flung it open, not even thinking to see who was on the other side.

"I brought you donuts and coffee. It's time to get started on your renovation. Today's the day, right?" Jessie Delaight held out the bag and coffee to his daughter.

Angel accepted the early-morning treats. "It's six in the morning and why are you here? How did you know I was starting the renovation today?"

Jessie took the bag back out of Angel's hand, opened it, grabbed a donut, and turned around to sit on the lawn chair outside the trailer. Angel stepped out of the trailer and sat in the other chair. Lifting the coffee cup to her lips, she inhaled the earthy scent of the fresh brewed liquid.

"It's a small town and I also talked to Henderson Travis. He said you called and asked if he wanted to help you today."

Angel gave her dad a shrewd look. "And you are here why?"

"To help, of course."

"At six o'clock? I told Henderson eight. And you told me you weren't going to interfere."

"I'm not. I promise. You tell me what to do and what you need help with, and I'll do it. No coaching on how to do something. I promise." He held up his cup of coffee next to his daughter's cup. "Let's toast to that."

"Okay Dad, but why are you here so early?"

"I miss the early-morning rise for work," he answered.

A scratching on the door of the trailer interrupted their conversation.

"I guess Blink is up too." Angel got up to let her out. The tiny kitten followed Blink out of the house.

"I guess you are keeping the kitten too?" Her father reached down to lift the kitten onto his lap.

"I hadn't planned on it, but it seems to like it here. Matthew said it was healthy. He took it to the vet for me, and then I picked it up the other night when I was at his house. I don't know, I never thought I'd be very good with animals."

"I guess you'll find out. Is this critter a girl or a boy?"

"Matthew said it is a *she*. I think I'll call her Magic."

"Why Magic?"

"Since she is black and I love magic. Everyone tells me I have a haunted house, and now I have two black animals. Maybe I need some black magic. I named Blink because she found a pink teddy bear and she was black. Magicians blink and make things disappear while using their magic. Maybe Blink and Magic will keep me safe from Orvis the ghost. Having animals and naming them because my house could be haunted is kind of weird, isn't it?"

Her father laughed. "It will be good for you to be out of your comfort zone for a short time. Moving here is certainly out of your comfort zone and mine too. Are you sure you don't want me to camp out in the big house or even in the carriage house until you get it done? I heard you had to call Barney the other night."

Angel stood up and threw up her hands. "Honestly does everyone know everything around here?"

Her father answered as a car drove up her drive. "It's a small town. At least I've heard that's what small towns are like. Are you expecting another early-morning visitor?"

Angel called to Blink. "Blink, come here, girl."

The puppy turned from scavenging through the overgrown flower bed by the big house and ran over to Angel.

"She knows her name already?" Lila Henshaw asked as she exited her car.

"She knows she gets treats if she comes." Angel bent over to give the dog a piece of kibble. "What brings you out here this early in the morning?"

Lila held up a bakery bag and coffee. "I see I'm too late. I was at the White House Eatery having breakfast, and I heard you were starting your renovations today, so I thought you might want some sustenance of sugar before you started. And I hear Barney thinks we know each other well so you can put in a good word for him."

Angel looked at Lila and then looked at her dad.

"What can I say?" Jessie turned to Lila. "I tried to tell her what a small town is like."

Lila laughed. "Get used to it. It's all about love. If they accept you, the support is outstanding, even when you think you don't need it. You will find out afterward it was exactly what you needed." She bent down to pet Blink and then sat on the ground next to her.

"I can get you a chair," Angel said.

"I stand all day," the medical examiner explained. "A little time grounded to the earth feels good. They are going to release the autopsy report today."

"I thought the case was already closed," Angel said.

"Ted said it was closed. I wasn't so sure because I just couldn't believe that Dixon would kill his sister and then take his own life all over that house," Lila answered.

"And now?" Angel asked.

"I found too much alcohol in him along with the sleeping pills. That combination led to his death, so I guess it was suicide and not murder. I must admit murder was a stretch. Not so strange when I was in the big city. I should have remembered that this is Whistle Stop and that's why I moved here."

"Was Dixon prone to drinking?" Jessie asked.

"I never saw him inebriated, but he could have been a closet drinker. We all have secrets. That might have contributed to the rage when he killed his sister and then he couldn't live with himself, so he took the sleeping pills. At least that is the theory," Lila answered.

"Case closed. I guess I don't have to worry about there being a murderer around stalking my house. What do they think the page from the book meant?" Angel asked.

"I have no idea. You will have to ask Ted or Barney. It looks like it's time for me to leave. You have work to do," Lila said, seeing Henderson Travis drive up and park alongside the driveway.

"I better put the critters inside." Angel picked up Blink and put him under her arm and then picked up Magic and put her under the other arm.

Jessie got up and opened the door while saying to Lila, "Are you sure you don't want to stay and help?"

Lila laughed and answered as she walked to her car, "It's a small town. I have a feeling you are going to have plenty of help."

Angel frowned as she watched Lila walk away. "What did she mean by that?"

Her father answered, "It's a small town."

CHAPTER SIXTEEN

Angel sat where the cars were supposed to park in the carriage house, trying to decide if she wanted to expand her renovations to the downstairs. Instead of housing cars, it could be turned into a great room. Her dad and Henderson were upstairs taking out the nonload-bearing wall to open up the area making it into a larger space. It was a warm day; the sun was kissing the earth with its warmth, so Angel had the garage doors open. She turned and looked out when she heard a car on the driveway.

Mayme honked the horn before parking the car under a weeping willow tree near the carriage house.

Angel walked out to greet her. "Don't tell me. You know how to use a hammer too."

Mayme laughed as she opened the door, turning to reach into the back seat and pull out a cooler and some tins covered with foil. "No, I brought lunch."

Angel put her hand into her pocket to pull out her cell phone to check the time. "I guess it is that time. But you didn't have to do that."

"That's what friends do. Matt will be along in a minute. He had to stop and change clothes."

Angel frowned. "He's coming to lunch?"

"And to offer some muscle."

"I didn't ask him to help. We can handle this by ourselves."

Mayme handed the cooler and tins to Angel. "I've got a folding table in the car. I'll go get it."

"I'll get it for you." Matt came out from around the side of the Airstream.

"How did you get here? I don't see your car," Angel said.

"I walked. It's not far and I cut through the yard." He went to get the table.

Mayme called up the stairs to the others. "Lunch time."

They could hear tools dropping and feet on the stairs.

"Don't you have a B&B to run?" Angel said to Matthew.

"Your dad is here, Charlie is out looking at property, and we don't have any other guests right now. No new ones arriving until the weekend." He reached into the cooler and took out the ham sandwiches and arranged them on the table.

Mayme uncovered the potato salad and baked beans and said to the crew, "Eat up."

"Do you have a day off from the library?" Henderson asked Mayme as he took the silverware she offered him.

"It opens at one. I'm going to see if I can find any newspapers in our archives that might give us a little information on your house, Angel."

"I'm hoping when we get to the renovation of the main house there might be some interesting finds in the walls," Angel answered.

"As in another dead body? I hope not," Henderson remarked.

"As in markings inside a wall or under wallpaper. Old newspaper used as filling somewhere in the attic. You never know. One house we did in Chicago had love letters stuck in a wall behind a window frame. We assumed so parents didn't see them. It was a steamy romance." Angel smiled as she remembered the letters.

"One time we found a pistol underneath a floorboard," Jessie remarked. "Turned out it was used in a robbery where a bank teller had been shot many years before."

"Or how about the time we found a diamond ring wedged in a crack in the plaster underneath a molding?" Angel asked.

"Yup, you never know what you might find." Jessie slapped Henderson on the back gently. "I'm sorry your wife was one of our finds."

"So am I, but this house held nothing but bad memories for her mother, and I'm not sure why. It wasn't anything she ever talked about. In fact, she never did say much about her great-grandfather or her grandfather. Her mother grew up in that house, but I don't know much about that. I respected her privacy. We all have things from the past we don't want to talk about."

A siren interrupted Henderson's explanation. They turned to see a patrol car pulling into the driveway.

"Did anyone call the police?" Angel asked.

"Maybe something's happening here that we aren't aware of and a neighbor called," Jessie answered.

Barney Pipe cut the siren and the lights before getting out of his car and walking over to the group. "Am I late?"

"Uh... late?" Angel asked.

"For lunch and to help. I have a few hours off. I brought my trusty hammer." He lifted up the hammer he carried in his hand.

"I think we have enough help, Barney. You know what they say, too many cooks spoil the broth," Angel said.

Barney crinkled his forehead. "You're not making broth, are you? I thought you were tearing down walls. Is Lila coming back?"

"No, what do you mean coming back? Have you been spying on me so you know she was here? And it's a figure of speech which means too many people will get in each other's way," Angel said.

"He's here. Let him stay. We can get done faster and get you in your temporary home so you can start the renovations on the big house. We could have it all done before Christmas—the big house I mean. Then I can stay in the carriage house when I come to visit," Jessie said.

"I must get back to the library. I'll let you know what they find. You can all get back to work. I'll clean this up," Mayme said.

"Come on, Barney, I'll show you what you can do." Henderson led the way up the steps. Matt and Jessie followed.

"Barney means well and he's a good policeman, just a little quirky," Mayme said before she left. "It looks like you've got more company." She nodded to the driveway.

"Do we have a sign somewhere that says open for business?" Angel said to the universe as she watched Mayme go and Charlie Mattson drive up. She walked to meet Charlie at his car before he could get out. "Mr. Mattson, what brings you by?"

"Hi there, little lady. I was just in the neighborhood and wondered if I could tour your main house. If you want, I can also pick up a hammer and help with the renovations, but I see you aren't working on the house."

"Again, I'm not your little lady. And right now we are working on the carriage house, but we've got it covered. I would be happy to give you a tour but some other time. I really need to get to work here."

Charlie's eyes were on the main house. "Yes siree, that is a fine property. Are you sure I can't buy it from you? Ma'am. Is that better? I really mean no offense, but women are to be treasured and you shouldn't be working like this. Let the men do the heavy work and you do the thinking. Those pretty hands are meant for lotion, not paint and hammers."

Angel sighed. "I'll remember that. Thank you, Charlie. Perhaps we can arrange another time later in the week. I'll call you at the B&B."

"I'll be waiting. You have a good day." Charlie saluted her before starting his car and leaving.

Angel watched his car disappear down the drive. Perhaps she was too hard on him. He meant well; he just wasn't used to the new way women liked to be addressed. After all, it might just be the small-town way.

IIIIIIII

"Angel, come up and look what we found," Matthew yelled down the stairs so Angel would hear him.

Angel sighed at another interruption. She had an idea and wanted the time to ponder the way the first floor of the carriage house would look if it didn't house cars.

The men were huddled in a group where the wall used to be in the second story. Henderson was holding something in his hand.

"What is it, gentlemen?" Angel asked.

Barney chuckled at being called a gentleman. "We found these journals. Looks like it could have been a diary. It was in the built-in cabinet in the corner. We pulled the cabinet out and started ripping it apart, and the journals fell out. There was a hidden shelf in the bottom, and these were snuggly pushed into the shelf."

Henderson handed one to her.

Angel paged through the book. "I love it when we find these hidden treasures, but these belong to you, Henderson." She held out the book to him. "After all, this house belonged to your wife's family."

Henderson shook his head. "No, I don't want it. Jeri said terrible things happened to her family in this house. She didn't elaborate. I'm not sure she really knew, just the fact her mother didn't want anything to do with her family, and she didn't want Jeri to have anything to do with them either. It's better if I don't know. It's been all I can handle dealing with Jeri's death and the fact her brother killed her. The only reason I'm here is because I thought it would be good therapy to change the persona of this house and property."

"I'll keep them for a short time in case you change your mind." She held out her hand for Barney to give her the other book.

"Do you think Lila will be stopping soon?" Barney asked.

"I doubt it. She was here once today. Why don't you call her and ask her what she is doing?" Angel suggested, her eyes twinkling with mischief.

"Aw, shucks. I can't do that. It might be against department policy," Barney answered.

"What's against department policy?" Ted Pangborn spoke from the top of the stairs.

"Nothing, boss. I mean Ted. I mean Chief." Barney stumbled over his words agitated at having been heard by his superior.

"What brings you by, Chief? Did you come to help too?" Angel asked.

"No, I came to get Barney. I need him to come on duty early tonight. Ezra Jenks Auction is tonight, and already people are arriving, so I thought another body on duty early might be a good idea."

Barney set down his tools. "I'm ready boss, I mean Chief. Last time we had an auction there was a free-for-all when Sam Jenkins and Ila Dickens tried to outbid one another. I had to step in before Ila bopped Sam over the head with an old baseball bat she bought."

"And I thought I was moving to a crime-free berg. Already there's been two suspicious deaths—sorry Henderson—and now a free-for-all," Angel said.

They watched Barney and Ted Pangborn maneuver their way down the steps.

"We're done here for the day anyway," Jessie said. "We need to get the walls put up for the bathroom and anything else you want done. Then we need the electrician and plumber to come in. This wasn't a hard teardown at all."

"I have some ideas for the downstairs I want to run past you, so the plumbing and wiring might have to wait until we get the downstairs ready for those improvements."

"When do you want us back here?" Henderson asked.

"Bright and early tomorrow morning. Just you and Dad." She made sure Barney and Matt heard.

"I want your opinion before we rip more things up."

"I'm crushed," Matt said. "But I have new guests coming tomorrow for a night, and I better get home to make dinner for my old guests." He looked at Jessie. "I think Charlie said he'd be back for dinner."

"He just left a short time ago," Angel said.

"He was here?" Matthew commented.

"Yes, he wanted a tour of the main house, but I told him he had to come back another time. And now, gentleman, you'll have to excuse me. I need to take these books to my trailer and change clothes. I'm going to an auction."

CHAPTER SEVENTEEN

It seemed to Angel the entire town of Whistle Stop was at the auction along with half the state of Minnesota. Apparently, auctions were a big draw. Angel hadn't been to any auctions except for those involving real estate.

As she meandered through the goods that would be offered, she looked over the crowd. Ted Pangborn was talking to Stacy Ambruster over by the edge of the property. Barney was following Lila Henshaw, trying to get her attention. Mayme was sitting in a lawn chair near the hayrack where the auctioneer was going to start the bidding, and her dad sat on the ground by her feet. Angel thought it was perhaps good he was in such good shape. Most men his age wouldn't be sitting on the ground because they couldn't get up.

"Would you like a number?" A man sitting at a nearby table held out his hand with a piece of paper in it.

"A number?" she asked.

"Don't you want to bid on something? If you do, you need a number."

"Oh, I guess I'll take one just in case."

"We need your name and your driver's license number plus the phone number."

Angel grabbed a pen on the table and filled in the details.

"Here you go, little lady." The man handed her the number 225.

Angel was about to correct him when she saw his smile and remembered this was a small rural town. It appeared men weren't versed in the ways of what not to say to a woman. She took the number and said, "Thank you."

Deciding to find a place toward the side of the rack so she could see, she turned and inched her way through the crowd to what she thought might be the best spot.

The auctioneer came to the microphone and began his instructions.

Angel felt something lightly bump the side of her hip. A woman in a wheelchair was hitting her leg. Angel stepped sideways to get out of the way. She felt the tap again. Turning around and looking behind her, Angel said, "I'm sorry, am I in your way?"

"Nah, I just wanted to meet ya."

Angel frowned. "Couldn't you have just said hello?"

"You were in front of me. How could I say hello when you were in front of me?" the woman answered.

"I would have heard your voice and turned around?"

The woman laughed. "Get over it. I didn't hurt you, did I?"

"No."

"Well then what's the problem? I'm Eudora Brown. I live down the street from you. I have the statue of a Viking in my yard."

Angel moved back so she was even with the woman. "I've seen that statue. Are you a Viking fan?"

"Nah, no football for me, but ya gotta be loyal to those Minnesota teams whether you like the sport or not. That's what us Minnesotans do."

"I'm Angel Delaight."

"I know who you are. Poor Jerilyn died seeing that you got the home of your dreams."

"Yes, I'm sorry about that, but I couldn't have known what would happen to her."

"That's true." Eudora nodded in agreement. "If ya stick around, that will be your legacy forever. Small towns have long memories. I'm still the woman that broke up Ed Roger's marriage."

"You did?" Angel gasped.

"I didn't, but his wife thought I did so she took a hammer to Ed's car and then came over and took a can of yellow paint to mine. All Ed did was give me a ride home from the grocery store. My car wouldn't start in the parking lot. He carried my groceries inside, and then he was nice enough to fix a door for me. He took off his suit coat and his shirt so he wouldn't get it dirty. When he left, he walked out the door, carrying his suit coat and buttoning his shirt. My neighbor, Jenny Shrill, saw him and told his wife and the rest is history. Once a story starts in a small town, it's hard to stop it and it has a life all its own. Your legacy lives forever. That happened fifty years ago. Just ask around and you will see that's what they'll tell you."

"You don't mind?" Angel asked, trying to talk instead of laugh.

"Wouldn't matter if I did; it wouldn't change anything. Just go with the flow, that's what I always say. It's always interesting to see how the story changes. Quiet. That's enough chatting. I need to watch the auction so I can bid." Eudora held up her number.

The two of them watched as items went up for bid and were sold. Angel wasn't interested until the auctioneer stood by a painting consisting of a garden filled with flowers with a small shed in the center. A small river ran through the background of the painting. She fell in love with the picture and the colors. It was large but it would be beautiful in the carriage house large room when it was finished.

The auctioneer explained the painting was done by the past owner of the estate. It was the only painting of his left at the time of his death. The other works by the owner had been kept by his children. Though not being of monetary value, the value was in the fact it was a painting by one of Whistle Stop's own, and that itself made it valuable. He started the bidding at twenty dollars.

A few people bid. The price was up to fifty dollars when Angel decided she wanted the painting. She raised her number like she had seen the other bidders do. She felt a pain in her leg. "Ow!"

"Why are you bidding against me?" Eudora asked as she pulled her cane back.

"Because I like the painting." Angel tried to listen to the auctioneer and raised her hand again. Again, she felt pain as the cane tapped her leg. "Why are you hitting me?"

"You're bidding against me," Eudora said.

"I'm not," Angel answered, trying to keep up with the bid. "You haven't raised your number."

"I don't raise my number. I just give ole Jeb the auctioneer an eye and a nod."

"An eye and a nod?" Angel looked at Eudora.

"I have clout, so if you know what is good for you, quit bidding," Eudora ordered. "I don't want to pay an arm and a leg for a painting that isn't worth anything that I'm giving for a gift."

"You better listen. You don't want to make Eudora mad. The consequences are some you'll never forget," Matt said to Angel as he joined them.

"Matt, grab her arm and don't let her bid. Darn it, old Hatty Elder is getting the up and up on this painting." Eudora yelled out to the auctioneer, "One thousand dollars!" She then held up her arm with the number.

"What happened to the eye and the nod?" Angel asked.

"Well, missy, you distracted me so I'm tired of the thrill of the chase, so I decided to end it." She raised her arm again and yelled, "One thousand and I'll throw in a pie for the losers."

"You bake? And I thought you and the auctioneer said this painting wasn't worth anything?" Angel stated.

The auctioneer said, "Going once, going twice—sold to the young lady in the wheelchair. One thousand dollars plus pies for the other bidders. Leave your numbers at the table, and Eudora will see you get your pies."

"Matthew, will you go and get the painting for me?" Eudora asked.

"I will." To Angel he said, "I'll also get your ticket for the pie since you were bidding, so don't go away."

"It's good you bought that old house," Eudora said to Angel. "It had a lot of sorrow. Not too many people know about it, and the ones that do—meaning me—aren't talking, but I can tell you it needs some happiness to bring it back to life."

Matt joined them and was about to hand the painting to Eudora so she could hold it.

"No, give it to Angel. It's my housewarming gift to her. It is sunshine and beauty and hopefully Angel will have sunshine and beauty in her life."

Angel took the painting, and a tear dropped from her eye, surprising even Angel as she wasn't prone to crying. "Thank you. I don't know what to say or why you decided to buy it and then give it to me."

"Why do you think I didn't want you to bid? You will have a bruise on that leg tomorrow. I knew the moment I saw that painting that it belonged with you. I have an intuition about that sort of thing," Eudora answered.

"Eudora isn't known for her charitable attitude," Matt said with a side wink at Eudora.

"He's right. And don't tell anyone. I've got to go and get out of here before this ole chair gets run over as I'm rolling home." Eudora put her cane in her hand and began rolling through the crowd, parting the people from time to time with her cane.

Angel watched her go. "Is she for real?"

Matt laughed and was about to answer when Angel knew what he was going to say. She laughed too. "I know. Get used to it; it's a small town."

CHAPTER EIGHTEEN

Angel wasn't used to walking home at night in the dark. On the Miracle Mile back home in Chicago, there were always people milling around at night. It was a mix of tourists, local people enjoying the nightlife, and panhandlers. Since she lived downtown, it wasn't unusual to walk to her favorite restaurant at night. There was plenty of light, and usually she had one of her friends with her as they all lived close in downtown condos and lofts. But here in Whistle Stop the streets were dark with the occasional streetlight illuminating her path. The shadows of the trees swaying and the sounds of the rural nighttime creatures and bugs were a different experience, and she tried not to let them spook her. After all, the locals said it was safe to walk the streets of Whistle Stop alone, day and night. But now with the shadows conjuring up images only imagined, she wished she would have taken the ride Matthew had offered.

Once she became comfortable with the quiet and the shadows, she savored the peacefulness of the night and the stars twinkling brightly overhead. It was not a view she was used to.

Walking past the main house, she thought she saw movement inside. She stopped to ponder whether she was brave enough to investigate or to call the police to check it out. Remembering her last experience, she decided she would check the doors to make sure they were locked before jumping to any conclusions.

Jiggling the lock on the front door, she found it was secure. Deciding to check the perimeter of the house, she stopped at intervals and jumped up like a jumping jack to see if she could see into the windows. Nothing moved inside the house so she continued on to the back door. It too was locked. It must have been the wind and the shadows from the trees, plus her wild imagination that made it seem as if there was someone in the house. Maybe it was haunted. Angel laughed, thinking that she was buying into the rumors.

After letting Blink and Magic out for a bathroom break and a little playtime before bed, she sat down to enjoy the rest of the evening, making sure Magic didn't go far so she wouldn't get lost in the shrubbery and trees. Blink always came back when she called, but Magic was too little to know that yet, and did cats ever come when their name was called?

Matthew was going to bring the painting Eudora gifted her over in the morning, or send it with her father when he came to work with her in the downstairs of the carriage house. Angel had never had someone she didn't know give her a gift. Eudora was certainly a character.

Blink made a growling noise. He was wrestling with something he found in the trees alongside the yard.

"Blink, what do you have? Bring it here right now."

Blink stopped his tugging, dropped what he was pulling, and ran over to Angel, hopping on her shoes so she would pick him up.

"One of these days you are going to be too big for me to carry you," she said as she scooped him up. Making sure Magic was busy with her toys underneath Angel's chair, she went over and picked up the object the puppy had been dragging. "Where did you get a child's sneaker?"

The bright pink little-girl's sneaker wasn't even wet from the dew on the grass. Angel put Blink down so she could examine the shoe. It was a bit worn but in good shape. Angel wondered if someone had dumped a bag of a girl's clothes and toys in her woods. Why would they do that instead of taking it to Goodwill? Soon she would have to examine the woods behind her home and the overgrown path that led to the creek winding around her property. It was on her list to do as soon as the carriage house was done.

Part of the woods would be cleared to make room for the new garage she planned on building since she was going to turn the entire carriage house into living space.

"Come on, Blink. It's time to go to bed."

Blink instantly went over to Magic and pushed her toward the door of the trailer.

"Blink, you seem to understand everything I say. Are you sure you aren't human?"

CHAPTER NINETEEN

The sun was shining when Angel woke up the next morning. Blink sat by the door, indicating he needed to go out. Rubbing her eyes, she opened the door, intending to step out with him to make sure he didn't wander too far, but when she took the first step, her foot ran into something hard and solid sitting in front of her door. Looking down, she saw it was an animal kennel.

"What in the world?" she said to the fresh air hitting her directly in her face.

Stepping around the kennel, she saw there was what looked like an adult black cat. Blink was already nose to nose through the kennel door while the cat, not being sure about the strange nose, was making soft hissing sounds.

A note was taped to the side of the kennel. The note was from Bridgette.

Angel, please keep this cat for a little while. We found it while we were hunting for strays last night. This one is very tame. It must have belonged to someone. We took a picture to search for its owner, but we are out of room at the shelter and have no more foster homes available. I thought of you. I didn't want to wake you. I'll check in later.

Angel put the note down and shook her head. Apparently, this was another small-town quirk. She moved Blink away from the kennel and put her fingers up to the door so the cat could sniff them. Instead of hissing, the cat put as much of its head against the bars as it could to rub her hands. Opening the kennel door, she picked up the cat. It immediately started purring and buried its head in her arms.

"I guess one more isn't going to hurt. What do you think, Blink? Let's introduce this one to Magic."

Blink followed Angel back into the Airstream. Magic was sleeping on Angel's bed, but when Angel set the new black cat down on the floor, Magic hopped off the bed to meet the newcomer. Angel grabbed Blink to keep him from interrupting the two.

The new cat sniffed at Magic. Magic immediately gave a short meow and then snuggled up right next to the older cat. They did look alike. Maybe Magic was this black cat's kitten, although Angel hadn't checked to see if the older cat was a girl or a boy. Satisfied that all was well, she put Blink down to see how he would introduce himself.

Blink sauntered up to the black cat, tail wagging. The black cat let out a soft hiss, but then Magic ran up to Blink and started licking his fur. The black cat sat back and watched and then sauntered off, jumped on the bed, and closed its eyes.

"I guess that's settled," Angel said to the animals. "It's time for my coffee."

Pouring a cup of coffee from the coffee maker she had set on a timer to brew before she woke up, she sat down by her small table to think about her day. Noticing the journals they found in the carriage house, she picked one up and started to page through it, thinking maybe she had time to read a few pages.

A knock on her door interrupted the thought. She heard her dad's voice. "Wake up, sleepyhead; it's time to get to work."

Putting down the journal and taking another sip of coffee, she stood up and sighed. "Coming, Dad," she said as she opened the door to join him.

"Late night? I saw you were at the auction last night. It looked like you were having an interesting conversation with the woman in the wheelchair."

"You could say that. I didn't see you bidding on anything. It looked like you were more interested in Mayme than the auction. Is there anything you want to tell me?"

Her dad laughed as he held the door to the carriage house. "Yup, it's time to get to work, boss. What are we doing today?"

"We are tearing down part of the wall by the stairs. I want to make the staircase wider eventually, but right now we need to open it up." Angel went to stand on the spot where eventually the steps would reach. She continued speaking while gesturing toward the wall that covered the stair risers. "Underneath the stairs is going to be a reading nook. I think the kitchen will be off to the back of the stairs, and the rest here will be an open room." She twirled around the room, her eyes closed while she imagined the space. Stopping by the garage doors she said, "I'm going to keep the garage doors but replace the wood entirely with glass." Angel patted the garage door. "It will be like the restaurants in Chicago where the walls open up so we can be outside but closed when the weather is cold or bad. I'll use drapes for privacy."

"That's kind of crazy, don't you think?" her dad asked.

"Coming from you? I've seen the glass skyscrapers with the glass overhangs that you have built."

"True, but this is just an old carriage house. Aren't you going a little too far with this if you are only going to live in it for a short time?"

"Matthew's B&B gave me an idea. I can do an Airbnb here after I move into the big house. I'm hoping to have all this done in a year or two."

Her dad looked around the room. "We could probably get this done sooner than that. I can call some friends, and it seems you have a lot of volunteer help from the citizens of this community, whether you asked for it or not."

"I guess that's what they do in small towns. That woman last night even bought me a painting. Actually, you were to bring it over today. Matthew took it home with him in his truck. I walked."

Jessie shook his head. "Didn't see a painting, but I haven't seen Matt either. He wasn't at breakfast. It was just Mayme and Bridgette."

"Speaking of Bridgette, she didn't say anything about leaving a black cat off here last night, did she?" Angel asked.

"Um, she did. She brought it back to the Brick Schoolhouse, trying to figure out where to take it. She couldn't keep it at the B&B because one of the guests was allergic and started sneezing the minute she brought it in," Jessie explained.

"What time was that? It had to have been late when she left it off."

"About two in the morning. We were up having a nightcap. Charlie Mattson is quite an interesting character. He's traveled the country. The new guest for the night was a retired FBI agent, female if you believe that, so it was an interesting chat. Not the usual small-town banter I've gotten used to in the past few weeks. I suggested Bridgette bring the cat here."

"Thanks, Dad," Angel said sarcastically.

They worked in silence for the next hour, only making small comments here and there.

"Have you been down to the creek yet? You might have to clear some brush before you can get there. Matt said it's pretty overgrown." Jessie wiped sweat from his brow.

"There is a tiny weed-and-tree-infested path, and I think it's probably more overgrown farther down. I decided to get this done and then take time to explore the property and area. The map was very detailed on the grove. There is nothing back there anyway, although Blink seems to keep finding things on the edge of the grove, such as a pink teddy bear and a pink little-girl's shoe."

"That's strange. Were they old?"

"No, they looked fairly new. I suppose some animal could have dragged it in from somewhere. I think I saw the eyes of a raccoon peeking out at me the other night. Aren't they known to scavenge?"

"Look at this, Angel." Her dad had just pulled off a section of wall underneath the steps, exposing the space.

Angel came over to his side. "It looks like a hiding place where someone stuffed memories. How did they get them in there?"

"Through the rungs of the steps. Look, these steps used to be open. Someone closed them up, but whoever put these things here must have slid them through the rungs, because this wall was solid."

Angel picked up what she thought looked like a crocheted blanket. "It's a baby blanket."

Jessie reached for a piece of cloth in the corner. "This is a home-sewn sleep shirt for a baby."

"Why would they stuff them down here?" Angel examined the blanket. "This is old, but it's beautifully done."

Jessie picked up all the other items on the floor. "They are all homemade baby clothes and blankets. All seem as if they've never been used. They're from a long time ago. Didn't someone tell you there were bad memories in this house?"

"They did. Maybe someone had a baby that died, and to help hide what happened, someone stuffed all this underneath the steps, thinking the clothes wouldn't be found," Angel surmised.

"And boarded up the steps, although why they wouldn't just throw the clothes away or donate them is beyond me," Jessie added.

"Grief does strange things," Angel said.

"It's time for lunch. Let's go to the White House Eatery. Why don't you get that pink shoe that you found, and we'll take it with us and ask if there is a lost and found in the community?"

"I left it by my chair outside the motor home last night," Angel said, stepping outside into the sun.

"We can finish the downstairs later today. We made good progress this morning."

Angel turned around to answer while making her way to the trailer. "Yes, then I'll get Henderson back here and we can frame the walls upstairs and the kitchen down here. Next we'll let the electricians and plumbers do their thing. I want to put a bathroom on both floors." She stopped in front of the Airstream and looked by her chair. "It's gone."

"The shoe?"

"Yes, I left it right here."

"Maybe Blink dragged it off again."

Angel looked around the side of the trailer. "He could have, but I'd swear I was watching him every second when he was out this morning. But maybe I got distracted."

"Black cats on your doorstep first thing in the morning will do that," her dad warned.

CHAPTER TWENTY

ila Henshaw motioned them over to her table the minute they set foot inside the White House Eatery. "Join me. I have room. It's the communal table at lunchtime."

"The communal table?" Angel asked as she sat next to Lila.

"We will commune by inhaling our food," Jessie answered as he took the chair across from them.

"Who knows who else will join us. We locals use this table for coffee, lunch, and whatever. Not that we don't sit at the other tables, but we leave them for the families, outsiders—I mean tourists—and anyone who is having a private lunch. There is nothing private at this table so beware," Lila warned them.

"Are you keeping busy? No more mysterious deaths in this town?" Angel asked.

"Quiet as a ripple in a pond," Lila answered. "I have been doing a lot of thinking about Jerilyn and Dixon. Why would Dixon try to kill Jerilyn by wrapping a wire around her neck? He wasn't the violent type. I remember once he fainted from the sight of his own blood when he accidentally cut his finger. I wish I would have remembered that and maybe looked beyond the signs that it was the heart attack that killed her. But then they did find the book by his body. It was open to the scene that was tried with Jerilyn before she had her heart attack."

"Did you find the cat?" Bridgette set menus down on their table.

"Don't you ever go to school?" Angel asked Bridgett.

"Work release. I have a study hall after lunch, so they let me help out here over the noon hour. It's more money I can donate to the shelter."

"I found the cat, but I can't keep it, only until you find a new home," Angel warned.

"We found it at the edge of your property by your woods. So we will check with your neighbors to see if it might be theirs or… you could do that. Get to know your neighbors," Bridgette suggested.

Angel answered, "Fine, I'll do that. Are you a neighbor matchmaker now? I think I'll have the special."

Jessie said, "I will too. Don't worry. We'll figure out a home for the new animal."

"Do you know that man sitting at the lunch counter?" Lila asked.

"I do know who that is," Angel said. "He's the homeless guy who was living with Dixon. He was at the funeral talking to Ted Pangborn."

"It looks like he might know someone else in town. That's quite a sack of food he just picked up," Jessie commented.

Angel got up and stopped the homeless man by the door. She stuck out her hand. "Hi. I'm Angel Delaight. We met at the funeral. I bought the old Stevens' house. I remember you were friends with Dixon Warner. I imagine you miss him."

The man tentatively reached out his hand and took Angel's. "Yes, I ah… ah… was an old friend of his. We worked together when Dixon lived in Minneapolis for a short time. We kept in touch and when I became down on my luck, he took me in. It's nice to meet you, but I have to deliver this food before it gets cold."

"You have more friends here in town?" Angel asked.

"No… ah… just some friends I brought down from the city from my workplace. I found a new job, and we are going to have a picnic in the park before we go back. I had some loose ends to tie up and it's always nice to have company on a drive." The homeless man pushed past Angel and disappeared out the door.

"Interesting," Angel said as she sat back down with Lila.

Bridgette brought their food. "He's a nice man. Comes in quite often and takes food out to his friends."

"He comes down from Minneapolis often?" Angel asked.

"At least once or twice a week; he always gets takeout. I never see him with anyone else, but then I'm not here all the time. Remember? I have to go to school. Speaking of which, I have to get back to class. Dotty will finish your table."

Jessie watched her walk away. "Busy gal."

"That she is. Her parents are hard workers too. I don't know what we would do without them. I have to get back to work too. Have you read those journals you found yet?" Lila asked as she left a tip on the table.

"How did you know I found journals? I know… It's a small town." Angel rolled her eyes.

"Actually Barney told me when he stopped at my office yesterday. He said he wanted to follow up on a hunch he had regarding Jerilyn and Dixon, but I think he just wanted to ask me to dinner."

"Are you going?" Angel asked.

"Only because he has me intrigued with his theory and wants to run it by me before he talks to Ted."

Jessie asked, "Why don't you just admit you want to have dinner with him? Women!" He threw up his hands in exasperation.

"Because I don't want him to get any ideas, but I also know when Barney has an idea, he can get himself in trouble and we all end up with more work. So I thought I possibly can head him off before his imagination gets the best of him. This was a simple case, although as I told you before, it seemed out of character for Dixon. You should have asked the homeless man that question since he knew him better than all of us, except for Henderson, and Henderson agrees with that too."

"It's time for us to get back to work too. Just a few more hours and my daughter's temporary home will be ready for the next steps—walls, plumbers, and electricians." Jessie stood up. "Come on. If we don't get to work soon, these old bones won't move and I won't make it back to the Brick Schoolhouse for Mayme's after-dinner pie."

CHAPTER TWENTY-ONE

ngel decided a quiet night was what she needed. Turning down her father's invitation to go to the B&B for dinner—or supper as they called it in Whistle Stop—she made herself a sandwich. Shooing the three animals outside, she picked up the journals, taking her food with her to sit and enjoy the beautiful evening reading and keeping an eye on the critters.

Watching to make sure Blink, Magic, and the new black cat stayed in the yard, she opened her book to the first page. Satisfied the animals were staying close, she began to read.

I can't believe they locked me up in here. I tried to keep everything secret for as long as I could, but I never imagined this is where I'd end up. How can my parents do this to me?

They say it is for the best staying here until... until... I can't even write it down on this page. My parents gave me the journal. They said it would be good to write out my feelings, but I don't want them to read this. How will I keep this journal from them when they know I have it?

The worst time is right now, at night. The light is fading outside, and I must be careful with the candles and lanterns so no one knows I'm here. But what if they did? What if someone found out? I wonder what my parents told my friends or other relatives. What would they say about what my parents are doing or what I did? My parents are right; I must stay hidden until this is over. I wonder if he misses me. I didn't even get to say goodbye. I wonder if he thinks I don't love him anymore. Will I ever see him again so he knows my heart is still with him?

I'm so sad. Good night, sweet moon. I can see your light through the small window high up on the wall. Is he watching too? Our moon will keep our love shining bright.

Angel closed the book. Maybe she shouldn't read it. These were someone's private thoughts, but whose and what did the young girl do to merit having been hidden in a garage? It sounded like her parents wanted to keep her away from someone, a boyfriend maybe?

She was about to open the journal again, curious about what happened to the young girl, when a man walked up to the driveway toward her. So much for a quiet evening, she thought.

"Hi there. Notice I didn't call you little missy," Charlie Mattson joked.

"Mr. Mattson, what can I do for you?" Angel asked.

"It was a nice night and I was out for a walk. I saw you sitting back here as I walked by and thought I'd say hello."

"I was just doing a little reading. Let me put my book in my trailer."

Angel found Charlie petting the dog when she returned. Blink was basking in the attention.

"Nice dog you have here," he said when she rejoined him.

"I seem to be accumulating animals. Everyone thinks I need a pet, and now I have three."

Charlie laughed. "It's a small town. I've visited a few of them in my time, and they watch out for their own."

"I have noticed that," Angel agreed.

"How about a tour of your big house now?" he asked.

"It's still not for sale."

"I've accepted that, but I'm interested in what you're going to do with it. I've been interested in the old architecture for a long time, and I don't like to see the old history torn down for something new."

"I find that interesting since you are a developer."

Charlie coughed. "Yes, well... um... that's what makes me my money, but this is what interests me."

"I just happen to have the key in my pocket. I was there earlier drawing up some plans. Let me put the cats and Blink in so they don't wander off." Angel grabbed Magic and called Blink. She opened the door to the trailer and put them in. "Where is that black cat? I'm in charge of it until Bridgette can find it a new home."

"I saw it over by the woods in the back of the carriage house. I'll get it for you." Charlie called to the black cat softly as he went to retrieve it. "Here kitty, kitty." He peered into the woods while picking up the cat. "What's back here?"

"I don't really know. It's so overgrown. I know my property meets the creek back there. It's on my list yet this summer, but I didn't see it as urgent to explore. I want to get this carriage house done and then I need to figure out where I want to put up another garage, and some of this might need to be removed."

"Why another garage when you have the carriage house to store your vehicles?"

"I'm turning it all into a living space. And I need somewhere to store my Airstream too," Angel explained as she put the black cat in the trailer.

"When are you leaving Whistle Stop, or did you find another property?" Angel asked as they walked to the house.

"I'm not sure. I like this town. It's friendly and there are some interesting people here, not to mention the things that have happened lately. I might stay on for a short time and take a little break from work."

Angel unlocked the back door, wondering if it was a good idea taking Charlie on a tour of the house on her own. After all, what did she really know about him. But he had been staying at the B&B and Matthew or Mayme hadn't said anything. They seemed to like him as did her father. Maybe she was prejudiced because he seemed to relegate women to the *little missy* category.

"Someone did a job on this porch." He ran his hands over the paneling covering the holes that had been the windows.

"They will be replaced," Angel explained. "This will totally be redone."

"Wow this kitchen needs work." He walked over to the wood cookstove. "This is a relic, but I could see this as a focal point in the kitchen for something."

"Yes, I think I'll keep it, but I'm not sure how I'll use it."

Charlie began to tap on the walls.

"What are you doing?" Angel asked.

"Just checking for hollow sounds. Old houses like this have secrets," Charlie answered.

"Do you have secrets, Mr. Mattson?"

"Don't we all?" Charlie answered, quickly leaving the kitchen and moving through the dining room into the living room. "Is this where they found the real estate lady?"

Angel followed and found Charlie underneath the steps in the former hidden room. He was already down on the floor checking the seat beneath the stairs, pounding on it with his knuckles.

"Charlie, what are you doing?" Angel looked at him with suspicious eyes.

"Seeing if the police might have missed something. That's the amateur detective in me."

"Should we continue the tour?" Angel asked.

Charlie stood up and walked into the part of the room that was hidden from the outside, ignoring Angel. He ran his fingers up the wall, seemingly lost in thought. Then he said, "I can see it would be easy to hide a body or two in here." He turned to look at Angel, but it was as if he were looking right through her.

Angel shivered as Charlie looked at her. It was time to end this tour.

"Is anyone here?" Matthew's voice came from the kitchen.

"Here, Matthew. We are here," Angel answered, relieved to hear another person.

Charlie shook his head as if to pull himself out of his thoughts. "Hey Matt, my boy. Angel was giving me a tour of this fine house."

"Yes, well, we should go on with it, don't you think?" Angel said.

"That's okay. It's getting dark and you have more company. I'll come back another time. Is there still some pie left back at the B&B? Suddenly I'm hungry."

"There is," Matt answered. "You don't have to leave just because I'm here. I like tours."

"No, no, I don't want to stand in the way of new love with you and missy here," Charlie said as he wandered through the kitchen toward the back of the house. Later, gator."

Angel and Matt watched as he disappeared into the kitchen, then heard the back door slam behind him.

"That was strange," Matt said.

"You have no idea. I'm glad you came when you did. I think it wasn't such a good idea to give him a tour by myself."

"Was there a problem?" Matt asked.

"No, but he seemed fixated on this room. It gave me chills."

A noise over by the fireplace distracted her from continuing. "What was that?"

Matthew turned and listened. "It sounds like it's coming from the fireplace." He walked closer and put his ear down by the wall. "Squirrels or mice maybe. It almost sounds like scratching. You should call an exterminator or put out some bait for mice and see what happens."

Angel joined him to listen. "It could be a bird. I've had that happen in other houses we've bought. I'll call someone in the morning."

Angel lifted her head and turned it to talk to Matt, finding he had done the same thing. She looked into his eyes as he moved closer. *Was he going to kiss her?*

Matt held her gaze for a minute and then pulled his head back and stood up. "I'll walk you to your trailer. I brought some wine and I thought we could sit outside, enjoy a glass and talk about your plans for the carriage house. Your father and Mayme seem to be holding court on Mayme's patio."

"They do seem to like each other," Angel said. "I guess we could sit outside too and figure out if we should be concerned about a budding romance."

Matt held the back door open for Angel. "It's time to *wine* about it."

Angel rolled her eyes. "Merlot or Cabernet?"

⊞⊞⊞⊞⊞⊞⊞

"Did you leave the door to your trailer open? I didn't notice it when I arrived." Matt asked as he and Angel approached her temporary home.

"I didn't. I distinctly remember closing the door, although I suppose it's possible the door didn't latch."

"Or maybe Mattson didn't leave but came over here to do a little snooping, and we interrupted him when we came out of the main house," Matt suggested.

"Why would he do that?" Angel asked.

Matt shook his head. "I don't know, although I like the guy, something is a little off with him and his supposed real estate deals. He doesn't seem to spend much time searching but instead walking the streets and having coffee at the White House Eatery."

"I was happy to see you when you came into the house. Charlie was acting a little strange and it made me a bit unsettled," Angel admitted while entering her trailer. "Where are my animals? It's going to be a long night if I have to look for them."

A scratching sound came from behind the closed bathroom door.

Matt opened it and Blink and Magic ran out the door and hopped onto the sofa.

Angel frowned. "I know I didn't leave them in the bathroom." To the cats she said, "How did you get in there, and where is the black cat?"

"She must have gotten out and ran into the woods. Wasn't she the stray that Bridgette just caught?"

"She was. I guess she will have to catch her again. But how did they get locked in the bathroom? Was someone in here?" Angel quickly looked down at the floor by the door. "The journals are still here, thank goodness."

"Is anything missing?" Matthew asked.

Angel took her time walking around her little home, pulling out drawers to check their contents. Shaking her head, she said, "No it appears all is here. The only thing missing is the black cat."

"Do you want me to call the police and report the break-in?"

"Technically they didn't break in. The door wasn't locked, and they might surmise I left it open, and since nothing is missing…"

"I'm going back to the B&B and see if Charlie had anything to do with this. Are you going to be all right alone?"

Angel nodded. "I'm a Chicago woman, remember?" Jokingly she said, "Maybe they just wanted the black cat."

Matthew was about to leave when he glanced at the journals on the floor. "Have you started reading them yet?"

"I just got started when Charlie interrupted me for his tour. It seems a young girl was held captive by her parents in the carriage house. I haven't gotten far enough to find out why or who it might have been."

"Really, that seems unbelievable. After all, it was Jerilyn and Dixon's grandparents' home. I think it was their family home. That would mean whoever wrote the journal was related to them."

Angel yawned. "That's a question for another day. The electrician and plumber will be here tomorrow. I'm going to stay out of their way so I may be able to read some more."

Matthew opened the door to leave but turned back and kissed Angel on the cheek. "Sweet dreams." He rushed back out the door.

Angel held a hand to her cheek. *Was she so tired that she imagined Matthew kissed her on the cheek? She must need sleep.*

CHAPTER TWENTY-TWO

Jim and Jack Stanton were early-morning risers. They were on Angel's doorstep at 6:00 a.m. Once she walked them through the carriage house, confirming what they had agreed upon when they'd first come out to inspect the job site, Angel went home. She intended to go back to bed after having tossed and turned into the wee hours, listening to every unique sound that came from outside.

She had just closed her eyes, only to have them pop open when she heard a tap on the door. Moaning, she got up and went to the door, intending to send whoever it was on their way.

"It's just me and I have coffee." Lila Henshaw stuck a cup through the opening of the door.

Angel didn't have the heart to send her away, and the coffee smelled too good to miss. "Lila, I didn't expect to see you."

Lila entered the trailer. "I have news. I see Jim and Jack are here. They are the best in the county, maybe even the state."

Taking a sip of the hot coffee, Angel indicated Lila should sit down at the small table. "What's the news?"

"Ted and Barney have reopened the investigation into Jerilyn's and Dixon's death."

"Really? What happened?"

Lila took a minute to answer. "I wasn't comfortable with the fact that Dixon killed his sister and then himself. In talking to all those who knew him, even though he was angry, they felt he wouldn't have harmed his sister. He was a teddy bear at heart."

"That's what everyone says, but doesn't everyone have a dark side?" Angel asked.

"They do, but I went back through the crime-scene photos and my notes. I saw some bruising around his jawbone. At the time, I didn't think anything of it. We weren't looking at it being a murder, and now I have a new theory. I think he might have passed out from the alcohol, and then someone poured the bottle of sleeping pills down his throat and held his mouth shut until they dissolved."

Angel spilled some coffee on the table, rattled by Lila's words. She quickly wiped up the liquid. "That's quite a theory."

"Though I can't exactly prove it, Ted decided to listen and do some more investigating, so don't be surprised if he is over checking out your home. I must admit Barney is very supportive of this conclusion."

Angel laughed. "Barney would be supportive of any conclusion you came to so he can get in your good graces. He is head over heels in something with you."

Lila nodded her head. "I know. I try not encouraging him, but he seems to be encouraged by anything I do."

"Poor guy. He's got it bad. Apparently, the feelings aren't reciprocated?"

"I can't see that he's my type. In a way, he takes after his namesake. He bumbles, fumbles, and is all over the place, a nervous nelly. Yet there is something endearing about him. He doesn't have a mean bone in his body; at least I don't think so. I don't know too much about him," Lila said.

"Ah… you are used to those city types. Suit, polished hair, and a good pickup line," Angel suggested.

Lila set her cup down on the table and stood. "You could have something there. What about you? I think Matt has his eye on you."

Angel blushed remembering the kiss on the cheek last night. "He's been a good friend since I've been here, but so have others. I have a house to renovate, and I'm not looking for any complications."

Lila opened the door to the trailer. "Speaking of complications, you have a black cat outside your door. What's up with all the black animals adopting you? Should I be scared? Are you going to put a spell on me?"

Angel followed Lila out of the trailer and stooped down to pick up the cat. "Something strange happened last night. After Charlie Mattson visited, I found my trailer door open, Magic and Blink were locked in the bathroom, and the black cat was missing."

The black cat meowed.

Lila scratched the cat on its head while Angel held it in her arms. "He or she is trying to tell you what happened. Don't you wish they could talk? Talking to our pets is like talking to someone from another country and we don't know their language. The only difference is we can learn another language, but I don't know anyone who teaches catspeak."

Angel asked, "Do you have a full day?"

"Every day is a full day. You never know who is going to present themselves on my coroner table."

"That's a scary thought."

"Not as scary as black cats appearing and disappearing. At least my bodies stay put."

❚❚❚❚❚❚❚

Angel settled down in the hammock she'd put up that morning between two sturdy-looking trees. Journal in hand, she closed her eyes for a few minutes to savor the peacefulness of the woods and the beauty of the warm day.

Taking one more breath of clean air, she opened her eyes and the journal at the same time.

Angel felt as if she was intruding on someone's life as she read the thoughts of a young girl, all alone and lonely in the carriage house with only her parents as visitors. Though she didn't seem bitter toward those parents, she seemed resigned to being there. A fate accepted, never mentioning her name or the name of her parents.

At least I have a treadle sewing machine and fabric. My mother was good enough to bring me yarn and knitting and crochet needles. She knows those things will give me something to do and keep me sane. I am very lucky at fifteen to know these skills. My mother taught me well. I suspect they too take her away from reality and her life with my father. I know he means well, but he doesn't know how to show that love to my mother or me. That is why he made my mother hide me here. If it got out, his position in the community would be tainted.

I love the blanket I'm crocheting right now. My baby would like it. No, I mustn't think of it as my baby because this child will not be mine. Father would be very upset if he knew I made things for this child. I have to make sure I hide all this when he comes to visit. I need to hide it from my mother too because it would make her too sad.

All they will see is the sweater I'm pretending to knit for myself and the dress they think I'm making, rather than the baby clothes.

Angel put down the journal. Tears fell on her cheeks. The child that lived in the carriage house had been pregnant. Who was she and what had happened to her baby?

She took the journal back into the trailer, deciding maybe to go back to the library to see what more information she could find on the house or talk to Henderson Travis to see if he knew any more of his wife's family's history.

A knock sounded on the trailer door. The clock on the wall showed almost noon. Putting the journal down, then having second thoughts about letting anyone else read it yet, she stuffed it under the cushion of the sofa before answering the door.

"Bridgette, what can I do for you?"

"Did you find the black cat I dropped off on my way to school this morning? We found it by the street by your driveway. I'm concerned that if it gets loose again, it might get hit by a car."

"You brought the black cat back? It got out because I must have accidentally left the trailer door open and someone put the other two critters in my bathroom, but the black cat disappeared."

Bridgett paused for a minute, trying to decide if she believed Angel's story. "Okay, I believe you, but this is a trusting cat. She belonged to someone, and we want to keep her out of harm's way until we can find her owner. We don't think she would fare well on her own in the world. So please double lock your doors when you leave."

Angel put her arm around Bridgette. "Bridgette, I promise I'll take care of the cat. I think it's amazing that a high school girl cares so much about God's creatures. Go back to school. I've got this."

"You should keep an eye on your dad too. I think he and Mayme have something going. Aren't they too old to make googly-eyes at each other?"

"Go to school, Bridgette. Let me worry about the *old folks.*" Angel pushed Bridgett out the door.

She was about to close the trailer door to go back to reading when the mail truck drove up her driveway. She waited until it stopped, then went out to meet the mailman.

"I don't recognize you. Are you new?"

"Yup, just transferred here from Apple Valley. Small town, you know. No traffic. Those on-ramps up in the cities got me confused. I always went *on* the off-ramp and *off* the on-ramp." The muscled, tall, and very thin man handed her a package.

"You must work out," Angel said as she examined the package.

"I can't have the only muscle that gets a workout in my head, you know. Nice place you have here. You live alone?"

"Thank you for the package although I don't remember ordering anything," Angel said, ignoring his question.

"I better get going. Even small towns have lots of mail."

"What happened to my other mailman? Did he get transferred to another route?" Angel asked.

The muscled mailman got back into his truck before answering, "I don't know. They said he just didn't come to work one morning. Lucky me. Have a nice day." He started the engine of the mail truck, gave a small wave, and drove down the driveway.

Angel examined the package in her hand. There was no return

address. She didn't remember ordering anything. Sitting down on the lawn chair outside her trailer, she tore open the box.

A photo album was nestled in the packing peanuts. Brushing the sticky peanuts off the album and lifting it out of the box, she opened the album, not sure what to expect.

The picture of a young girl stared up at her on the first page. Did she know the girl? The pictures seemed to be taken in recent times.

Angel turned the page. There was a picture of a woman, the little girl, and an older teenage girl. Next to the little girl was a black cat that looked suspiciously like the cat Bridgette kept bringing back to her.

Why had someone sent her this album? Angel picked up the empty box and examined it. There was no return address, only today's postmark.

A scratching noise interrupted her thoughts. Blink had woken up from his nap and wanted out.

The black cat followed Magic and Blink out of the trailer. She stopped by Angel's chair, jumped up, and settled nicely in the spot Angel had just vacated.

"Whom do you belong to, Mrs. Black?" Angel asked while reaching down to pet the cat, wishing she could talk in catspeak.

The cat licked her hand. Angel sighed. "I guess that's a conversation for another day."

CHAPTER TWENTY-THREE

"I'm Angel Delaight, and I would like to talk to someone about the package that was delivered to me yesterday." Angel addressed the woman behind the counter at the Whistle Stop post office.

The woman raised her glasses up on her nose and peered at Angel. "Was the material inside the package broken?"

"No."

"Was it damaged in any way?"

"No."

"Did you have a problem with where the package was left?"

"No."

"Was your mail carrier rude to you?"

"No."

"Was the package late?"

"No."

The woman plopped her hand on the desk and said, "Then what exactly is your concern?

"There was no return address, and I didn't order it," Angel answered firmly.

"Maybe it was a gift."

"There was no return address and no card."

"Then it was an anonymous gift. It happens."

"But I need to know who sent it."

"Didn't your mama tell you to not look a gift horse in the mouth? Was there something hazardous or dangerous in it?"

"No."

"Then what exactly do you want me to do?" The woman took her glasses off and stared at Angel.

"It had a postmark on it." Angel's tone was hopeful.

"So?"

"It came from Minneapolis. Is there no way to track it?"

The clerk sighed. "Do you still have the package with the postmark on it?"

"I do."

"Do you want to call the police?"

Angel frowned. "The police?"

"They can lift fingerprints off the package." The clerk smiled. "But if it wasn't dangerous, they might not cooperate with you."

"No, I do not want to call the police. Can I talk to my mail carrier?"

The clerk raised her eyes in frustration. "What is your name again? I'll see if they are here."

"Delaight. Angel Delaight and I live off Cricket Road."

"Don't recognize that address. Name of the former tenant?"

"I believe it was the Stevens' house."

"Did you know that house is supposed to be haunted?" The clerk backed away from the counter a little as if Angel were the ghost.

"You know where I live, not by the address but by the former tenant's name?" Angel queried, amazed at the way this postmaster found people.

"It's a small town," the clerk answered. "Let's see, that would be the new mailman, Ralph Kringle. He's not in right now; he's out on the route. I'll have him drop by. Although if I can't help you, I'm sure he can't either."

"Nice to know. I think I'm off to see the wizard or maybe I just visited the wizard," she said quietly as she left the post office.

CHAPTER TWENTY-FOUR

"What brings you by this morning?" her father asked as she joined him for a cup of coffee at the Brick Schoolhouse Bed-and-Breakfast. "I was just ready to come over in a little while to help with the Sheetrock in your little temporary house."

Mayme poured Jessie a cup of coffee before turning to Angel. "Would you like some too?"

"No, thanks, Mayme. I actually came to ask you and Matthew a few questions."

"I think Matt was headed to your house, little lady." Charlie Mattson joined them at the table. "Good morning, folks."

"My house? What is it with these early-morning visits?" Angel asked.

Mayme laughed when her father said, "We might ask you the same thing although it is almost eight forty-five, so not so early."

"I went to the post office. I received a mysterious package in the mail yesterday." Angel pulled the photo album out of her bag. "This was in it with no return address or clue as to who the sender was. And apparently since it isn't a bomb, the post office can't help me. Mayme, do you recognize these girls?"

Mayme sat down next to Angel and looked through the pages. "I can't say that I do. Are you sure this was meant for you?"

"It was my address, but my name wasn't on it," Angel answered.

Her dad stood up and moved behind Mayme to look at the pictures. "Not anyone I know."

Charlie Mattson had been listening to their exchange before reaching across the table and pulling the photo album in front of him. He was silent as he paged through the book. He went through it twice before closing it. "I can't say I recognize any of them."

Angel watched Charlie's expression. It appeared he might want to say more, but instead, he pushed the album back to them. "I hate to leave you all, but I found some very interesting properties yesterday and must be off to do a little more digging on their history."

"Have you decided yet how long you are going to be in town?" Angel asked, thinking he might have made a decision since their last conversation.

"Maybe indefinitely. Lots of interesting historical buildings here. You never know what they might develop into. Good luck purchasing your property today, Jessie." He took another swig of coffee before nodding to them and leaving.

Angel looked at her dad. "Your property?"

Mayme stood up and grabbed the coffeepot. I think I should make some more coffee. We have new guests coming soon, and I like to give them fresh coffee when they arrive. And you better get back to your house soon, Angel, or you will miss your surprise."

Angel watched her leave. "What kind of surprise and what property?"

Jessie shrugged his shoulders. "I don't know about the surprise, but I'm buying acreage outside of town by the lake."

"And you were going to tell me this when?" Angel's eyebrow arched.

"When the deal was closed. I kind of like this little burg, and it feels good to be out of the city. I'll be able to take up fishing and maybe have some animals on a hobby farm. Who knows what else I might have up my sleeve?"

"This doesn't have anything to do with Mayme?"

Her dad blushed. "It's too early to tell, but I thought it might be nice to be close to you and to retire here. You don't mind, do you?"

Angel looked at her father's handsome face. He seemed too young to retire. He wore his age well. "Not if you don't interfere with my plans?"

"Speaking of plans, what do you think that album might be all about?"

"I have no idea, but I guess I'll go and see what my surprise is and pretend amazement to find Matthew is at my house. Maybe he'll recognize these faces. Sheetrock installation will start at 11:00 a.m. sharp, so don't be late. Why don't you call Henderson and see if he can help? I have some questions for him too."

"Don't you want to practice your surprised look for me before you leave? You were never good at subterfuge."

"That's what you think. Remember the old VW Beetle that Chad used to drive?" She was referring to a former construction crew member at their business.

"Yes," her dad answered.

"I'm the one who forklifted it on top of the shop."

CHAPTER TWENTY-FIVE

ngel could hear hammering as she walked into her driveway. When winter set in, she wasn't going to be walking. Just the thought of cold weather made her shiver. She felt the urge to buy a car, a fun car, saving her truck to use in the winter and only for construction. It hadn't been practical to have two vehicles in Chicago. In fact, when she was at her condo, she left the truck at the construction company and took the L.

As she got closer to the carriage house, she stopped. The hammering wasn't coming from the carriage house but somewhere to her right, in the direction of the backyard of the main house. Looking over toward the noise, she saw something was being built in the back corner of the yard near the trees.

Changing direction, she jogged across her lawn to see who was doing what and why.

"You weren't here, so I got started with your surprise." Matt Harkins put down his hammer.

"My surprise? It is a surprise. I had no plans for this corner of the yard. What are you doing?"

"I'm building you a screened-in gazebo with a swing inside."

"Why? I didn't give you permission to do that."

Matt came closer to Angel. "It was something I wanted to do. I had the idea the other day when I saw you sitting on the lawn chairs by your trailer. You needed somewhere to dream and read that would be more comfortable until you get the carriage house and the main house done. I thought every woman needed her dreaming spot. And… it's going to be screened in so the flying critters we know as mosquitos won't get you."

Angel moved away from Matt and walked around, inspecting the area. It will be a nice addition to the property but why would you do that? I'm almost a total stranger to you."

"It's a…" Matthew started to answer.

Angel laughed and finished the sentence. "I know it's a small town."

"That's part of it," Matthew said. "The other part is I miss remodeling my bed-and-breakfast and I needed a hobby break, so I decided this would be my hobby, plus you might let me spend some time with you in the gazebo. I have squatter's rights since I built it."

Angle blushed. "I might consider that. Right now I have to change and get into my work clothes. The wiring and plumbing are done in the carriage house, so we are going to Sheetrock today, starting at 11:00 a.m."

"Carry on. I'll keep creating here." Matt waved her off with his hands.

Angel turned to walk away and then turned back. "I need to buy a car. Where is the best dealership?"

"Do I have a deal for you," Matthew joked. "When we conclude our work today, we'll get ourselves cleaned up and I'll take you out for dinner and we'll car shop."

"Don't you have to be at the Brick Schoolhouse?"

"My day off. Mayme is handling things with a little help from Bridgette. Six o'clock?"

"I'm not sure we'll be finished by then. Can we play it by ear?"

"I'll check in with you around five."

Angel hesitated for a second before saying, "That sounds good, and thank you for this." She nodded toward the pile of wood that would become her gazebo.

"Maybe the gazebo is the way to your heart and not my cooking?" Matthew smiled.

Angel, flustered, turned and practically ran to her trailer, thinking she wasn't ready for what this small town may have to offer.

CHAPTER TWENTY-SIX

Angel stepped down from her ladder and stood back, surveying the walls in the upstairs of the carriage house. "It's starting to come together."

"You doubted us?" her father asked.

"She thinks we are a couple of old coots," Henderson Travis answered.

"I don't. But I didn't think we would get this much done today," Angel explained.

"Should we tackle the downstairs today too? We could work late into the night," Jessie offered.

"I think we should call it quits for a day and have something cool to drink. I actually want to talk to you about the first journal we found the other day, Henderson."

"You think I might know something about it?"

"I have no idea, but the young girl writing it went through a very serious life event right here in this house, and I would love to figure out who she is."

"I don't hear any more pounding outside," Jessie said. "Matthew must be taking a break too. Should I be worried he has designs on my daughter? It's not every day someone builds you a gazebo."

"I do have designs on your daughter," Matthew said as he came up the stairs. "I'm calling it quits for the day too." He looked around at the walls. "Impressive."

"What he means is that he has designs on my time," Angel explained. "He is taking me car shopping."

"No, that's not what I meant, but I *am* taking her car shopping. You will have to wait for that chat with Henderson another time."

"She doesn't like to be told what to do," Jessie warned Matthew.

"No woman likes to be told what to do," Henderson added.

"Was I telling you what to do?" Matthew asked Angel.

"You were, but I have a suggestion. Why don't Matthew and I go look at cars as soon as we clean up, and then meet you all somewhere for a drink? It's time I visited some other local haunts. Whistle Stop must have one. I imagine, Dad, that you have plans at the B&B for dinner. We could eat and you could have a drink or dessert. Bring Mayme with you. Henderson, would that work for you?"

"You didn't ask me," Matt said.

"I didn't the same as you didn't ask me about the plans." Angel smiled.

"Touché," Matt answered.

"I'll ask Mayme. Where shall we meet you and what time?" her father asked.

"How about eight? We know where to meet you." Henderson added, "It's Our Little Secret."

Angel frowned. "Why is it your little secret?"

Matt answered as he grabbed her hand to pull her down the steps. "That's the name of our local watering place. Our Little Secret."

"And it's the best-kept secret in town," Henderson yelled after them before turning to Jessie. "You know what they say about secrets."

"No, what?" Jessie asked.

"That's my secret to know and yours to guess."

CHAPTER TWENTY-SEVEN

"I guess this place *is* a well-kept secret," Angel said to Matt as she looked around the bar.

"It's an out-of-the-way place with a few legends attached to it too, but I'll leave that for another time. Are you happy with the jeep you bought?"

"I am, although I wasn't planning on something so sporty. I have my truck too. Who needs two vehicles?"

"Apparently you," Matthew answered with a glint in his eye.

"It's a small jeep, and the top and doors come off. I didn't always want to run around in my big truck. I used that for my construction job and to pull the Airstream. I may sell them both if I decide to settle in."

The bartender sauntered out from behind the bar and came over to their table. "What can I get ya?" He peered closely at Angel. "Ain't you that new gal that bought the haunted Stevens' house?"

Angel chuckled at the word haunted. "I guess I am, and you might be?"

"Ralph. They call me Ralph the elf because I'm so short."

"Nice to meet you, Ralph the elf, although your ears are too tiny for an elf," Angel kidded.

"Cute ears, aren't they?" Ralph joked. "You saw Orvis the ghost yet?"

"I can't say I have," Angel answered. "I've seen a few shadows at night up at the house though, so maybe he's flitting around."

"Watch out there. It was probably Orvis that got mad because his house was being sold, and that's why he offed that real estate lady. What can I get you?"

"That's enough, Ralph. You don't want to scare the lady out of town, do you?" Matt warned.

Ralph laughed. "Sorry. I was just joshing you, but I can't see Jerilyn's brother killing her—or himself for that matter. They had their issues, but there was a strong bond between the two."

"I'll have a Minnesota Mistake," Angel said.

Ralph frowned. "What's a Minnesota Mistake? I've never made that one."

"I just made it up. It's whatever you decide to make me, and if I don't like it, I call it a Minnesota Mistake. It'll be a surprise," Angel said.

Ralph nodded his head. "You got it."

"You didn't tell me you see shadows at night," Matthew said.

"I don't always, and I think it's the movement of the trees reflecting the streetlights off the windows."

"Evenin', folks," Jessie said as he and Mayme and Henderson joined them.

"Hi, Dad. Mayme, it's nice to see you, and Henderson I'm glad you can join us," Angel said.

"I'll get us a drink. What would you all like?" Henderson asked.

"Why don't you have a Minnesota Mistake?" Matt suggested.

"And what might that be?" Henderson asked. "I've never heard of it, and I've lived in Minnesota for a while now."

Jessie, knowing his daughter's sense of humor, said, "Go to the bar and ask the bartender for a Minnesota Mistake. If he is already making one for Angel, he will know what to do." He could barely hold in his laughter.

"Got ya. A Minnesota Mistake for all?" Henderson left to order the drinks.

"It is so good to see you, Angel," Mayme said. "How are the renovations coming?"

"We are almost finished with the carriage house. The next step is to build me a big garage a little farther back in the property to house my truck, my trailer, and my new car," Angel explained.

"You bought a new car?" her father asked.

"Kind of."

"Kind of?" Her father's eyes lifted up when he looked at her.

"I bought a small jeep."

"Attagirl," Mayme remarked. "I always wanted a jeep but never had the courage to buy one. What would they say if an old woman like me cruised around town in a bright red jeep?"

Jessie looked at her. "Mayme, this isn't a side of you I've seen. A red jeep? Do you want to go hang gliding next?" he joked.

Mayme stiffened her shoulders. "Maybe. There's a lot you don't know about me, Jessie Delaight."

Ralph and Henderson put the drinks on the table.

"Let me know how you like your Minnesota Mistakes," Ralph said, leaving before they could taste their drinks.

"He left awful fast," Mayme said.

Henderson took a drink and began to cough.

Mayme sipped her drink and said, "Oh my."

Jessie, used to whatever surprises his Minnesota Mistake held, put the glass to his lips and carefully tasted the concoction. He remembered that in Chicago, Angel called these drinks Chicago Mistakes.

"This is actually quite good," Angel said.

"Down the hatch," Jessie said as he took a gulp without trying to taste the liquid.

"What is this?" Henderson asked.

"Mine looks different from yours," Mayme said.

"That's the Minnesota Mistake," Jessie answered. "They are all different and the bartender put something he normally wouldn't put in whatever drink he decided to give you. Now, if you don't like it, you can tell him he made a Minnesota Mistake. If you do, then drink up and name it and it will become your private drink."

Angel decided it was time to get down to business, so she said to Henderson, "The journals we found were written by a young girl who was kept in the carriage house by her parents during her pregnancy. It's a sad tale of being young and her parents not wanting anyone to know. She spent her time knitting and crocheting and sewing, making baby items that I suspect were the items we found sealed underneath the stairs. Do you have any idea who this young girl was? Did Jerilyn ever mention this to you or who in her family might have had a child out of wedlock as they called it in those days?"

Henderson took a moment to answer. "No she didn't. Her mother was estranged from her parents, and she didn't have any brothers or sisters. Jeri always told me her mother said terrible things happened in that house, and she didn't talk much about her grandparents at all. It was a surprise when she found out her father and mother actually still owned the house. Dixon never said anything either, although he did visit his grandparents from time to time. He was forbidden to go there, but he ran into his grandmother one time in town when he was a teenager, and she asked him to come over and not tell his mother. I remember Jeri saying when her mother found out, after talking to Jeri's dad, they decided Dixon was old enough to make up his own mind about his grandparents."

"How did it fall into ruin?" Jessie asked.

"Once Jeri's grandmother and grandfather were gone, Jeri's mother wanted nothing to do with that place. Why she didn't sell the place is beyond me." Henderson explained. "When Jeri's dad died, she was surprised to find they still owned it. After a few months she decided to sell it and hoped someone would buy it that would banish the bad karma in the house."

Mayme shook her head. "Such a sad story and to think a young girl was kept prisoner by her parents. What that must have done to her. What happened to the baby?"

"Maybe the rest of the journals will have the answer. I hope to finish them soon."

"Have ya hung the painting yet? Or haven't ya got that old haunted house up to snuff yet?"

They hadn't noticed Eudora wheeling up to them from the other side of the room.

"Eudora, it's good to see you," Angel said. "And no, I'm waiting until the carriage house is done to put the picture up."

Eudora tapped the leg of Angel's chair. "Didn't want to leave without saying howdy. I see you've met Ralph the elf. Leave him alone. He's mine. I don't want another pretty girl turning his head. Watch her, Matt. Too many Ralph's in this town for my liking. It's a good thing one is short and one is tall."

"Do you know another Ralph?" Mayme asked.

"Oh, that new doozle dinkle postman. He's always getting my mail wrong. I got a package from nowhere, sent to nowhere that he delivered. He claimed he had the wrong house. How could he have the wrong house when there was no return address and no address where it could be delivered? Mail delivery is getting stranger and stranger. I see you are all drinking Minnesota Mistakes. I stopped at the bar before I joined you. The bartender warned me there were weird folks at this table. He made me a sample. Great drink."

Before they could answer, she tapped her cane quickly again on Angel's chair and wheeled away.

"She is a strange person," Angel remarked.

"She might be able to tell you something that we can't," Henderson suggested. "She's been here all her life, and her family is from here. Maybe she knows what young girl might have disappeared for a few months all those years ago. Jeri's mom's parents couldn't have been the ones holding a girl hostage. Maybe a family lived in the house before them."

"I'll go through the archives of the library. Have you read the book on the history of the house that you took out of the library?" Mayme asked Angel.

"Oh my goodness. I forgot I had it what with the renovation and deaths and animals showing up and disappearing from my house. It must be overdue. You should have said something sooner," Angel said.

"That's fine. Keep it as long as you want. It's not a hot commodity," Mayme answered.

"I don't know about you, but I think I want another Minnesota Mistake." Henderson held up his glass. "I think after our discussion we are all going to need it."

"Ralph, another round of Minnesota Mistakes and then you better provide cab service home." Jessie downed the last drop out of his glass before waving it in the air to get the bartender's attention.

CHAPTER TWENTY-EIGHT

Angel sat in the gazebo, gazing at the night sky. The past couple of weeks had flown by since the night out at Our Little Secret. The carriage house was waiting for the final touches before she could move in. Matthew had finished her gazebo and was working on one of his own for behind the B&B. When she'd questioned Eudora, Angel found her knowledge of Angel's property was limited, although Angel suspected she wasn't being entirely truthful. Finally finding the time to read the history of her house from the library book, it seemed the Stevens' family had always owned this house. It went down through generations. The book offered no clues to who the journal writer might be.

Life fell into a routine of work and trying to figure out how the black cat kept getting out and disappearing. Bridgette kept bringing it back, always threatening to find it another home. The shadows in the house at night seemed to be just that—shadows. She hadn't found anything more in the house to suspect human or ghostly visitors except once in a while the bathroom faucets seems to drip, but she had her plumber check them out. He said they were old and probably sensitive to the vibrations in the house. She didn't quite believe that, but since she would be working on the house soon, she let it go. Maybe it was Orvis the ghost. Of course, she could have the water turned off until she started her renovation, but Jerilyn had explained when showing her the house, they hadn't turned off the electricity or water after finding out they still owned it, wanting to make sure things were all in working condition before listing it for sale.

Hearing a crunch on the driveway, she stiffened until she saw Matthew coming into view of the gazebo. "I didn't expect to see you tonight."

Matt sat down beside her. "It was a nice night for a walk, and I wondered if you used this at night. After all, I wanted to make sure I didn't do all this work for nothing."

Angel answered, her face crinkling into a smile. "You certainly didn't. I love it. It is perfect and I sit here in the mornings and watch the sun come up, and in the evenings it's my peaceful spot."

"Where are the furry creatures?" Matt looked around.

"In the carriage house. They love the space now that it's almost done. I couldn't coax them outside tonight. They were all passed out on the fur rug by the french doors upstairs."

"Is the black cat still here too, or has she disappeared again?" Matthew asked.

"So far she is spending her night with me. She is an escape cat and must have figured out how to maneuver door handles. All the doors are locked tight. I have the key right here." Angel dangled the key from her hand.

Matt took the key from her and put it on a ledge on the side of the wall. "Is this the key to your heart too? Should I see if it works?"

Angel knew if she could see his eyes in the darkness they would be twinkling. "It doesn't unlock easily."

"Then maybe I need to soften the lock."

"And how would you do that, Matthew?" Angel asked teasingly.

"Like this." Matthew leaned in and gave her a light kiss on her mouth. "And what's with the Matthew? I thought we agreed on Matt; most people call me Matt."

Angel was going to respond when out of the corner of her eye she saw a flash of pink by the Airstream. "Someone's over there," she said, jumping up and running out of the gazebo.

Matt followed.

Angel stopped when she got to her trailer. "Hello there," she said cautiously to the small girl in the pink dress. "It's dark. Should you be here? I haven't seen you before."

The little girl backed up and seemed ready to run when she saw Matt.

"It's okay. He won't hurt you," Angel said to the small girl. "What's your name? Are you lost?" She bent down to look into the girl's face.

The girl in pink lowered her eyes to the ground and scuffed the dirt with her feet. "No."

"Does your mom know you are here?"

"No."

"Maybe you should come with me and we will take you home. Where do you live? It is pretty late for you to be out." Angel stood up and offered her hand.

"It's okay. She's my sister. I'm supposed to be watching her, and she got away from me while I was out hunting for stray cats and dogs." A teenage girl came up from the side of the trailer.

"And you are?" Matthew asked.

"I work with the rescue group that Bridgette works with. Sorry she bothered you. We have to get going. My mom will kill me if she knows I kept my little sister up past her bedtime. Come on." She took the little girl's hand.

"It's nice to meet you. Are you sure I can't give you two a ride home?" Angel asked.

"We're good. Bye." The two hurried down the driveway.

Watching them leave, Angel said to Matthew, "That was strange."

Matt still had his eyes on the girls until they turned at the end of the driveway onto the street, then disappeared. "That it is. I'll have to ask Bridgette about that." He turned to Angel and put a hand on her cheek. "Where were we?"

"We were talking about locks, which reminds me I need to unlock the furballs and bring them to the trailer. I don't want them spending the night until I'm there with them. They like to cause trouble and rearrange my knickknacks."

"Can I help?"

Angel reached up and gave Matthew a kiss on the cheek. "The lock has softened a little. I think I can manage it alone. Tell my dad to be here bright and early so we can finish up. My furniture is coming on Saturday."

CHAPTER TWENTY-NINE

Angel unlocked the door to the carriage house. She immediately felt a breeze across the room. The window was wide open and the screen all the way up. Looking around for a weapon in case she wasn't alone, she picked up a brass candlestick sitting on the fireplace. Having discovered it along with the baby clothes underneath the steps, she had decided to keep it as a memento of the history of the carriage house.

Grasping the candlestick, she flicked on the light switch, illuminating the downstairs. Cautiously she checked the bathroom and the closets. She still hadn't seen her animals. She switched on the stairway lights and took the steps quietly and cautiously, the candlestick ready. At the top of the stairs she hit the upstairs lights. All seemed to be in place, even Magic and Blink who were still dozing on the fur rug.

They certainly weren't going to be watch animals. She silently chuckled at the thought, as they hadn't stirred when she stepped into the room. Quietly she continued her journey checking the bedrooms, bath, and closets. No one was hiding anywhere. She looked around. She couldn't see anything missing except the black cat. Should she call the police? Not wanting to have to answer questions from Barney Pipe or the police chief when nothing was missing except the cat, she decided to let it go.

Nudging Blink and Magic she said, "Come on, time to go home and go to bed."

Downstairs, she examined the open window. There was a piece of fur on the edge of the screen. Who had let her out? Or had she left the window open? Had that been why the little girl and the teenager were here? Or had it been someone else? What was going on?

She checked to see the windows were all locked, then shooed the animals outside and waited for them to do their evening relief exercises before herding them into the travel trailer. "Soon we can stay in the carriage house."

She turned around taking a final look before locking the carriage house door. All seemed peaceful and quiet.

Feeling a little unsettled, she decided tonight would be a good night to finish the second diary. The girl's pregnancy had progressed with the doctor always visiting the young girl in the upstairs of the carriage house. The girl passed her days knitting, crocheting, and making baby clothes and dreaming about the child's father, hoping he would rescue her and they could keep the baby. Whoever this young lady was, she loved her child, and had it not been for her parents, she would have moved hell and high water to keep it.

Angel settled into bed and opened the last few pages of the journal.

My baby is almost here. Sweet Lily, I'll love you always. I'm sure you are a girl even though I don't know for sure. I won't know until you are here and I see those tiny toes and beautiful eyes. I hope someday someone finds these journals, after my parents are gone, and they find you so they can tell you that your mother loved you beyond her own life, and she loved your father, but circumstances forced us apart. I'll give all that I made for you to the doctor so he can give them to your new parents whoever they are. They are made with love. I don't want this. I want you. I will never forgive my parents for this. Maybe I should have fought harder to get out of here, but I had to think of you and take care of myself for you so I could give you life.

I have to be quick. My mother is here so they would know when I started having pains. I have to write my last pages and hide this journal with the other one. You are letting me know you want out in this world. I haven't been able to write as much with my mother here because she has been watching me, but right now she is fetching the doctor. I love you, sweet Lily. We will meet someday in another life. I will never forget you as long as I live. Your mother, always and forever.

Angel put down the book and wiped the tears from her eyes. Had the baby been a boy or a girl? What happened to the mother? Did she ever find her baby again? Why were all the clothes hidden instead of having been sent with the doctor to the baby's new home? Where was the baby and who was the girl from the journal?

Angel knew she had to find out. So far Henderson had no idea. There had to be clues somewhere in the old house about who this young girl was. Or in some old papers somewhere. The only link left to this mystery seemed to be Jerilyn's husband, Henderson, as he and his son were the only living relatives even if it was by marriage.

Angel snuggled deeper into her bed. First things first, a good night's sleep, getting moved into the carriage house, and building a new garage. Then work on the house could begin, and maybe, just maybe, she could bring some peace to the spirit of the young girl who gave up so much at such a young age.

CHAPTER THIRTY

When Angel opened the door the next morning, the black cat sauntered in as if it hadn't left, meowing at her as if it were scolding her for leaving it outside all night.

Magic and Blink passed the black cat. As she came in, they went out.

"I better follow you to make sure you don't disappear too," Angel said to their backs. The black cat settled on her bed.

"I guess you're in for the day." She turned and gave it a pat before walking out the door, shutting it tightly behind her.

Her father was just coming up the driveway. "I think I can finish up alone if you have errands to run."

"I do have a few things I want to check. Tomorrow is the day they're delivering my furniture, and I want to make sure they will be here at nine sharp. Maybe later this afternoon we can bring some things in my trailer over to the carriage house."

"We can do that, but why don't we celebrate tonight at Our Little Secret? There are no new guests coming tonight at the B&B. We can invite Charlie to join us. He's a little strange but seems to be a good guy. Invite Lila and Barney too. I'll call Henderson. I'm buying."

"Wow, is there a catch?" Angel asked her father, wondering where this excitement of celebration was coming from.

"You are moving to the carriage house and starting your garage next week, which makes it closer to your working on the house, and I'm closing on my little spot of heaven on the lake. Who would have thought us big-city people would want small-town life?"

Jessie reached down to pet Blink. "She sure is growing. They can stay with me in the carriage house while you're gone. Where's Black Cat?"

"Black Cat?" Angel noticed that her father had dropped *the* in front of black cat.

"We can't keep calling it *the black cat*. She appears like she is going to stick around, so I named her Black Cat," Jessie said.

Angel sighed. "Yup, your reasoning hasn't changed. She's in the trailer. If she doesn't want to come out now, you can let her out when you take a break. I was reading the last of the journal last night, and it brought me to tears. I have to find out who this young girl was. Maybe tonight I can talk more to Henderson about it to see if he might have forgotten something."

"I best get to work. Don't forget to tell Matt, or better yet have him pick you up." He left for the carriage house before Angel could answer.

Angel went back into her trailer to get her purse. As she reached for it, the photo album that had arrived mysteriously in the mail got caught in the shoulder strap and fell to the ground. Angel reached down to pick it up. It was open to the page of the picture of the two girls. Picking it up, Angel studied their faces. These were the two girls she met here last night? That was it. The photo album was delivered to the wrong place. It was supposed to go to the home of the girls, wherever that was.

She decided to take the photo album with her and stop at the White House Eatery. Maybe someone there would know who the girls were and where their family lived so she could get the album to the right place.

Backing out of her driveway with her truck, she was glad she was picking up her new jeep next week. It wasn't quite as big as the truck or as noticeable, or maybe she wanted an excuse to buy a new vehicle. Ralph the mailman was at her mailbox delivering letters when she left. Angel took the time to stop and roll down her window. "I think I know where my package was supposed to be delivered. Well, I almost know. The sender had the wrong address."

Ralph nodded. "Gotcha."

Angel pulled into the full parking lot at the White House Eatery and eased into a spot next to the dumpster. As she stepped out of her truck, someone tapped her on the shoulder.

"That is a mighty big truck for a little one like you," Charlie Mattson said.

Angel raised her eyebrows.

Charlie took one look and backed away. "I'm sorry, Angel. I didn't mean anything by it. I know, I know. It's not correct to talk to women that way anymore. But Angel, it's a big truck. How can you see anything without cranking up that seat? You have to jump to get down. Your daddy should have had something custom built for you when you worked for him. You were one of his employees, and I would have done that had I had a daughter."

Angel shook her head. "Charlie, that would have been favoritism, and we didn't believe in that at Delaight Construction. We all had to pull our weight whether we were related or not."

"Fine, I'll try to do better. If I do, can we be friends?" He stuck out his hand.

Angel looked him straight in the eye and hesitated for a minute. "No more little lady? No more girly girl? No more comments about my fragility because I'm a woman?"

"No... or I'll try. It's hard to teach an old dog new tricks, you know."

Angel took Charlie's hand. "I seem to hear that a lot in this town. We've got a deal."

"Can I buy you breakfast as a truce?"

"You can. I have some investigating to do."

Charlie held the door open for Angel. "I hope opening the door for you isn't too much?"

"I think I can handle that, Charlie. In fact, it's kind of nice."

Lila was sitting at a table by the window and motioned for them to join her. "We meet again."

"I was going to call you. Dad is taking us all out for dinner to celebrate tonight, and he told me I should invite you and Barney. You too, Charlie."

"Are you trying to set me and Barney up? Doesn't he do enough of that?" Lila asked.

"No, I swear it was my dad's idea, but he did mention you and Barney in one breath."

"I hope he held it because it will be a long breath. Barney and I are working colleagues. No more, no less," Lila said.

"What's that you have in your hands?" Charlie asked, indicating the photo album.

Before Angel could answer, Bridgette set coffee down in front of the newcomers. "I figured you'd want coffee, so I just brought it." She took the menus from under her arm and set them in front of Angel and Charlie. "Lila had our triple meat omelet with cinnamon toast. It's delicious."

"Bridgette, I met a teenager and her little sister last night at my house. Her little sister snuck away from her and ended up by the trailer. The teenager said she was helping your rescue group when the little one managed to elude her."

Bridgett crinkled up her nose. "I don't know who that would be. We weren't out last night. I had to do the family thing with my parents and decided to go to bed early. Did she say what her name was?"

Angel took out the photo album. "I'll do you one better than that. I'll show you a picture. They were younger in this picture, but I recognize them. Somehow this album got mailed to me by mistake." She opened the book to the picture of the two girls.

Bridgette took the book from Angel's hands and studied the pictures before closing it decisively. "Nope, I have never seen these two girls. Are you sure it's them and are you sure she said they were from the rescue group?"

"I am. And by the way, Black Cat, as my dad calls her, got out again last night but this time by the window in the carriage house. I don't know how that happened. Either she is able to open doors and windows or a ghost is letting her out."

"It's Orvis. I knew it. It's Orvis," Bridgette declared. "We need to do a séance or a ghostbuster. Aren't you scared?"

"Calm down, Bridgette. I'm sure there is a reasonable explanation for all of this," Lila said.

"You're into dead people. Shouldn't you agree with me?" Bridgette asked.

"It's time to take our order. I'll have what Lila had. I have to get to work as my moving day is tomorrow." Angel gave her the menu back.

"Me too." Charlie handed his menu to Bridgett. "We'll talk again about having an exorcism. It might be interesting. I might have to hold a few in some other properties I own." He laughed at the expression on Bridgette's face as she walked away.

"How long are you going to be here, Charlie?" Lila asked.

"I'm not sure. I have some properties I'm investigating, but nothing has been finalized yet." He turned to Angel. "I don't suppose you want me to see your house now? I'm sure it has gone up in value now that you've finished the carriage house."

"Why do you want it so badly, Charlie?" Angel asked.

"It intrigues me. Maybe that's why I'm sticking around and don't want to admit it. I keep hoping you'll change your mind. It's a hunch; a feeling that all is not what it's supposed to be. You need to be careful."

Lila studied Charlie's expression. "Are you warning her away? That's a strange thing to do. But she has nothing to worry about. The investigation has finally been closed on Jerilyn and Dixon. We have our suspicions but nothing we can prove. Dixon read that book that he left, decided to try to murder his sister that way, or maybe he was just going to threaten her with the wire, and then she had a heart attack and died. Dixon was so distraught he drank too much and took too many pills. It's time to move on."

"I'm glad you got it sorted out. So you think the book put ideas in his head?" Charlie asked.

"It might have just been a coincidence he chose that way. It's a popular book, and no one else seems to have murdered anyone because of it."

Angel stood up. "Will you excuse me for a minute? I want to show these pictures around to the other customers to see if they recognize these girls so I can get this album to the right family."

"We'll let you know when your breakfast comes."

Angel sat down at the counter and opened the album to the page that had the pictures of the two girls. She called the other waitress over to the counter. "Do you recognize these two?"

"No, I've never seen them."

Angel turned on the stool and looked around the room. The homeless man was sitting in the corner in a booth hidden from the rest of the room. She could just make out his face partially blocked by a coat hanging on the coat hook on the booth. She walked over to the booth.

"Hi, do you remember me? We met at church at the funeral?"

The man looked up and just nodded.

"It's nice to see you back in town. Are you living here?" Angel asked.

"Just visiting friends. I'm taking them some food. Here it is now." He took the takeout bag from the waitress who had just looked at Angel's album.

"I was wondering"—Angel set the album in front of him—"while you were living here with Dixon, did you ever see these girls?"

The homeless man looked down at the page. He slammed the book shut, stood up, and said, "This isn't any of your business. Leave it alone and don't show this book to anyone else or you'll be sorry." He pushed past Angel and left by the side door.

Angel, a little shaken from the man's demeanor, made her way back over to the table and joined Lila and Charlie.

"What's the matter?" Lila asked. "Your face is as white as a sheet. Did you find someone who knows the girls?"

"Um, no. I… ah… will keep looking."

"Was that the man who used to live with Dixon who you were talking to? Did he upset you?" Charlie asked. "He left quickly."

"No, no. I'm fine. It's just I realized how lucky I am to have a home. I think he's taking food to some homeless friends. We've seen him do that before in here."

Bridgette came over to their table. "Thanks for going out tonight. I get the night off from the B&B. I think Mayme and your dad might have an announcement, but you didn't hear it from me. When are you and Uncle Matt going to make an honest niece out of me?"

CHAPTER THIRTY-ONE

Angel surveyed the lower level of the carriage house. She and her dad moved her belongings over from the Airstream and put them away. Her new kitchen purchases were tucked away in the cupboards, waiting to be used. All that was left to be moved in was her furniture and appliances, and they would arrive tomorrow.

Twirling around in happiness, she collapsed on the floor and was immediately joined by Blink, Magic, and Black Cat. They tussled in fun for a few minutes before she thought she caught a glimpse of pink run past the window that looked out toward the woods. She quickly got up and peered through the glass, looking in both directions. Maybe it had been a reflection off her new bird feeders she'd put up outside the window that afternoon. They were red, but maybe her eyes played tricks on her and made them pink in the reflection.

"Time to go, kids. One more night in the trailer and that means you too. I'm going out to celebrate and find out if Bridgette is right, that Dad and Mayme have a secret announcement. Hopefully in their old age they haven't went off the deep end and decided to jump into a permanent relationship."

The animals followed her out the door. She turned and locked it. They must have understood what she said because all three of them were waiting to get in the trailer. Once inside, they had a little skirmish, deciding who was going to sleep where on her bed before settling down.

She chose a printed and to-the-floor bohemian-style dress with dangling loop earrings and rope sandals to wear to Our Little Secret. Pinning her hair on top of her head, she whirled around in the mirror to make sure she was all put together. It felt like she was in another world, so she wasn't sure if her style of clothing would fit small-town Minnesota, but then that was her goal, to find her own style and her own life.

"Sleep tight, girls." She patted each animal before picking up the journals off the table. Angel decided it was time to share a snippet of the young woman's words with the group.

Stepping outside, she took in a breath of fresh air. A small whiff of something caught her nostril and the smell took her breath away. What was that? It certainly wasn't a clean air smell. She looked around. Had someone dumped a Porta-Potti on her land?

An SUV came down the driveway and stopped behind her truck, blocking her in.

"You might as well ride with us," Matt shouted through the open window. "It's safe; Mayme and your dad and Charlie will protect you."

Angel walked over to the SUV. "Do I need protection from you?"

"Sweetheart, you better believe it," Matthew answered before getting out of the SUV and opening the passenger-side door for her.

"I don't need to hear that," her father commented from the back seat.

"Where did my fresh air go?" Angel asked, sniffing the air outside the SUV again.

"That is the aroma of money," Matthew said. "Haven't you seen the pig operations peppering our countryside? Someone must have spread some manure on the fields this afternoon. They use it for fertilizer."

Angel sniffed again. "I think I prefer the smell of the crisp green stuff better."

Charlie was ignoring the conversation, staring at the house as the

SUV backed out of the long drive. "Are you sure you have your house locked? I could swear I saw movement from inside."

Angel glanced at the house. "I thought that many times too but have concluded it is just the way the trees reflect on the window. At night it is almost ghostly. The police have been here twice and found nothing, so I deduced it is either Orvis or the tree sweepers."

"I understand the excitement starts tomorrow at 10:00 a.m.," Mayme said. "I'll provide lunch for all the friends who are helping you get the place in order. It will be exciting to have help arranging your new furniture and appliances."

Angel frowned. "Help? I think it's just me and the delivery people."

"If you say so," Mayme answered.

"We're here and it looks like the others are as well." Matthew nodded his head toward their friends who were entering Our Little Secret.

Once inside they were led to a small room off the bar and dining area.

"We have our own room?" Angel commented.

"I thought we could party without interruption here," her father answered.

"Dad, I've seen you party hardy. It's not very loud. No offense. You party the elite way; the Chicago-style. prestigious champagne-and-caviar way."

"It's time I let my hair or what's left of it down a little."

"I'm scared." Angel sat down on one of the chairs at the table.

The rest followed suit. Barney made sure he was next to Lila. Henderson parked himself at the end of the table. Matt joined Angel on her side of the table. Charlie took a seat next to Matt. Mayme sat on the side of Lila but left a space between her and Lila. Jessie sat down at the opposite end of the table from Henderson.

"I know I work with dead people, but I promise I won't autopsy you," Lila said to Mayme, indicating the empty chair next to her.

"We invited someone else, but she isn't here yet. We invited Bridgette too, but she had another engagement. She said she could catch up on how we behaved the next time she works at the Our Little Secret," Mayme answered.

Angel lifted her head and looked at her dad. "How would she do that?"

Charlie wiggled uncomfortably in his chair. "Girly, oh… I'm sorry, Angel, haven't you learned anything yet since being in this town? Even I know that."

Angel rolled her eyes. "I know… it's a small town."

"I took the liberty of ordering drinks for everyone," Jessie announced when the waiters came in with champagne.

"I didn't know they even knew what champagne was at Our Little Secret," Henderson commented.

Lila and Barney had been silent up until now.

"Turnin' into a speakeasy, are you?" Barney suggested.

"Barney, do you even know what a speakeasy is?" Lila asked.

"No, but I know think they had something to do with drinks you hadn't served yet."

Lila laughed. "Barney, you need to read to brush up on your laws. They were establishments that sold alcohol when it was illegal."

"Well, we don't have champagne flowing out of faucets here— I mean, it's not usually something we can order so… I don't know. You just make me nervous, so I blurted it out."

Lila patted his arm. "Relax, Barney. No autopsies on you tonight."

"I would like to make a toast if Lila and Barney have determined I've broken no laws." Jessie held up his glass.

The rest of them followed.

"To new adventures, new relationships, and future risks." Jessie looked at Mayme, tapped her glass, and they both took a drink.

Angel's eyes were wide when she turned to Matthew, questioning him with her look. He shrugged his shoulders but poured another glass of champagne and gulped it down, worried about the next words that would come out of Jessie's mouth.

"And what new adventures might those be?" Angel asked with trepidation, worried that he and Mayme were going to announce an engagement.

"Yes, I would like to know that too," Matt added in a stern voice.

"Whatever it is, I think we should be prepared with another glass of champagne first." Henderson held up his glass, trying to break the tension he felt coming from Angel and Matt.

"You can't announce anything till I get seated." Eudora briskly used her cane to walk into the room and over to the empty chair. Barney quickly got up and pulled it out for her.

"You can walk?" Angel asked.

"Of course I can walk, but it's easier to get around in that wheelchair since I broke my dadgummed leg. It isn't quite healed. Just because I'm old doesn't mean I'm decrepit, but it had its advantages. They always let you sit in front at an auction, and it's easier to tool around town in a wheelchair rather than my car—saves on gas too." Eudora sat down. "Now you can make your announcement."

Angel frowned. "You know about this?"

"Of course I do. I arranged it," Eudora answered.

"You arranged for Mayme and my dad to get together?"

"You arranged for them to get engaged?" Matt belted out.

The entire table became silent, their glasses seemingly frozen to their lips waiting to see what was going to happen.

"I'm here. I just found out. Oh-em-gee! Oh-em-gee! I can't believe this is going to happen, and when I found out you were going to make the announcement tonight, I had to be here. I can't believe I turned you down when you invited me. Oh my gosh! Where's a chair?" Bridgette grabbed a folding chair from the side of the room, opened it, and plopped down on its seat.

Angel looked at Matthew and frowned before whispering to him, "Can't we stop this? They haven't known each other long enough. And at their age, don't you think they would have more sense?"

Jessie cleared his throat loudly. "As I was saying before we were interrupted…"

A knock sounded on the open door. "Excuse us, but we heard you were here and were going to make an announcement, and we were wondering if we could cover it for the *Old Whistle Stop Times?*"

"You called the paper?" Angel asked, disbelief in her voice.

"No, I did," Bridgette said. "I thought it was very newsworthy."

"My dad and your great aunt getting engaged is newsworthy?"

Bridgette eyes became little slits when she looked at Angel. "Engagement, what engagement?"

"Enough." Jessie's voice rose so everyone would hear him.

Mayme was giggling and she tapped his shoulder. "They think we are engaged. Engaged?" Her giggle turned into a full-blown guffawing.

Angel said to Matt, "I'm confused."

"If you would all let me continue, Mayme and I are engaged to go into business together. As you all know, I bought the acreage on the edge of town by the lake. We are turning it into a bed-and-breakfast animal ranch. Bridgette has convinced me there is a shortage of good care for homeless animals. Mayme and I are going to give them a home until they are adopted. We will take in more than just cats and dogs. We will give them love, vet care, and adopt them out."

"Yes, there is a small barn on the property we are converting to my living quarters. The main house will become Jessie's living quarters but remodeled so that he has his own home inside the bed-and-breakfast where people can stay. Hopefully they will want to adopt an animal when they leave."

"You're going to compete against me?" Matthew asked.

"Yes and no. It will be an entirely different experience. Yours is more upscale and more for those who want a fine weekend experience. Ours will be more hands-on. The visitors can help with the animals' care," Mayme answered.

"Dad, what do you know about animals?" Angel asked. "We never even had a pet."

"I have hired our own veterinarian, and Joe from our construction company has signed on. He was raised on a farm, and he worked at and was a board member of the humane society. He actually has a lot of experience in that field. Who knew? He wanted a career change," Jessie explained.

"The announcements have been made, so let's order," Eudora interjected.

Angel turned to Eudora. "How do you fit into this since you knew about it?"

"My son is the veterinarian he's hiring. I came up with the idea and pitched it to your father."

Charlie patted Eudora on the back. "Have you ever tried selling real estate?"

"Why, Mr. Mattson, are you flirting with me?" Eudora winked at him.

Charlie laughed. "When I'm flirting, you'll know it, little lady."

Angel sighed at his use of *little lady*.

"I for one think it's a great idea. This dinner is also a great idea. Now that the announcements are over, let's celebrate," Charlie said.

The waiter came in with the first course of their meal.

Henderson frowned, looking at his plate. "Since when did Our Little Secret serve the meal in courses? This is a bar and restaurant. The old hole-in-the-wall, out-of-the-way place."

"Oh, I forgot to tell you. I bought this place too," Jessie answered.

"What!" Angel stood up. "Are you buying up the entire town? I moved here for a quieter life, not for this town to become the Delaight Project. You promised me you wouldn't interfere with my life."

"Settle down, settle down." Charlie Mattson was about to add little lady but thought better of it. "I found out the owners wanted to expand their menu but were having trouble raising the capital for the project. I put your father on to it, and he visited with them. They decided the best way to do this and provide a decent income for their family was for your father to invest in the business, pay them a salary to run it, and any profits over the payment he makes to the bank and any repairs that might have to be made, goes to them. This seven-course meal is a test to see if they can pull it off and offer it on special occasions to customers who ask for it."

Angel signaled to the waiter standing at the door. "I need a Minnesota Mistake, a strong one after all these surprises."

The room quieted down. Lila and Barney concentrated on their food as did Angel and Matthew. The rest of the conversation between the others flowed easily.

Finally Angel turned to Matthew. "Did you have any idea about any of this?"

"I didn't. I'm still speechless. They all kept it a secret from me. I don't know what Mayme was thinking, or maybe I'm just worried about myself. She helps out with everything at the B&B. I can't believe she would do this to me. We are going to have to have a good heart-to-heart in the morning, and if she's moving to the acreage, what about her house?"

Henderson nudged Angel. "It'll all work out. Your dad needs something to keep him busy. You can't go from running a company to being totally idle, and your project isn't going to last forever."

"On another note," Angel said to Henderson, "I finished the last journal. Henderson, do you have any idea who this young girl was that was kept in the loft of the carriage house to have her baby? Her final entry was heartbreaking." Angel took the book out of her purse and opened it to a page in the middle. She began to read.

"I felt the baby kicking today. I imagine you are here with me feeling her movement too, and I see your smile. You would be so happy. Are you looking for me? I know I am young, but I know I love our baby, and I know I would be a good mother. My heart is breaking because I will never get to rock him or her at night; although I have a feeling it is a girl, our Lily. I will never get to watch as she takes her first steps or sees a butterfly for the first time. But I will remember these moments forever when she lets me know she is here in the dark of night, and I'm not alone, and she is alive and waiting to make her mark into the world."

The room had become quiet. The others, hearing Angel reading, stopped talking and listened. When she finished, she said, "It doesn't matter how many times I read this, my heart breaks each time. I have to find out who this was and what happened to her baby."

Henderson's eyes were wet. He shook his head. "Jeri never said anything. She couldn't have known what happened in that house, and her mother, if she knew anything, never let on to any of us."

"It had to be someone from your wife's family, Henderson." Eudora spoke with a shaky voice, her eyes, too, wet with moisture.

"Maybe I can look back through the files and see if any baby died about that time. It might be in the archives of the morgue," Lila suggested.

"Well shucks, I can do a little snooping too. I'm sure the chief wouldn't mind. See if anything is in the old police papers in the basement. It wouldn't be on the computer because we didn't go that far back," Barney offered.

"Maybe you should just forget about it," Jessie said. "Leave the past in the past."

"Maybe Orvis isn't Orvis but this girl's spirit haunting your house," Bridget said.

Charlie didn't say anything, just listened and jotted some things on his napkin as if he was doodling.

"I can't do that. I can't leave it alone," Angel answered.

"Henderson, didn't you say one time that after Jerilyn's grandmother died, her father had to go over and go through things in the house, and though his wife had told him to get rid of everything, he did bring some boxes home to store in his attic in case his wife changed her mind?" Eudora asked.

Henderson thought for a moment. "I guess you are right. I forgot that. I haven't touched anything in the house yet of Jeri's. When her father died, she hauled the stuff from his attic to our attic to go through sometime, but she died before she could do it. I guess now is as good a time as any to see what's up there. I'll look."

"How did Jerilyn and Dixon's mother die?" Angel asked.

"She fell down the steps of the carriage house. A board was loose, and her foot caught it and down she went. She hit her head and never woke up."

"Was there anyone living on the property at the time of her death?" Matt asked.

"No. Jeri's mother didn't want anything to do with that house. She had it boarded up. That was why it was so strange when they found her mother there. After her mother died, Jeri's father kept the house but kept it boarded up. When he died, Jeri reopened some of it so she could clean it up a little from years of neglect to sell it. Dixon actually started making some repairs. He spent quite a bit of time over there until she put it on the market. That's why it caused so many problems. Dixon wanted that house," Henderson explained. "Why? I have no idea."

"Why didn't she just let Dixon have it?" Lila asked.

"Because her father stipulated that the house must be sold. They weren't to keep it, and she wanted to honor his wishes," Henderson answered.

"No offense bringing up bad memories," Barney said, "but that might be why Dixon murdered Jerilyn and took his own life. The bad luck of the house rubbed off on him, and he couldn't live with himself after he killed his sister. Yes siree, and then there was that book he was reading, *The Thin Red Line* by that Justin Young fella. Yup, gave him the idea to try to kill Jerilyn; maybe he just lost it. Books like that shouldn't be in the hands of those that are unwell."

Charlie stood up and pushed back his chair, which made a loud scraping noise, interrupting the conversation. "I hate to break up this party, but it's getting late. Matt, I can call a ride if you all want to stay later."

"No need," Angel said. "Matthew, I really should be getting home. It's a big day tomorrow."

"We're ready," Jessie said. "The news is out; let the excitement begin."

CHAPTER THIRTY-TWO

"It looks like you're all moved in from top to bottom," Matthew said to Angel as he surveyed the downstairs of the carriage house.

"It does. I wonder how it will feel to sleep in an actual building again instead of my Airstream?"

"It looks like the animals have made themselves at home, at least Blink and Magic. Where is Black Cat?"

"She is probably wandering. I'm sure Bridgette will bring her back tonight. I think she should give up with the idea that Black Cat is going to be anyone's pet. That cat seems to be an escape artist and have a mind of her own."

"When are you starting with the garage?" Matthew asked, looking out the large picture window into the yard of trees.

"Soon. I have my workers all lined up. I'm hiring a crew from Dad's old construction company to come out from Chicago. I know and trust them. It's worth the cost. They are going to do it on one of their weekends. I want to get it done before the snow flies. First I have to investigate the woods and get a few of the trees cleared. I want to make sure I don't ruin the woods but have the garage blend in. And I need to clear the path down to the creek. It would make a nice walk in the woods for meditation."

Matthew thought for a moment. "I can help you with that."

Angel answered, "Yes, as I have learned from my carriage project and this morning's move that in a small town you have lots of help. I was amazed at everyone who showed up to help. It took a matter of hours to get everything moved in and decorated, and all I had to do was supervise, and the food Mayme provided was over the top. What are you going to do without her?"

"We chatted about that a little this morning. Apparently, this critter ranch has always been her dream, but she could never afford it, so your dad provided the land and the money, plus she has always wanted to live by the lake. Your dad apparently wants to get involved too—with the ranch, I mean, not Mayme."

"That doesn't solve your problem," Angel pointed out.

"I'm happy for her, and I cook as well as Mayme. She taught me everything she knew so I just need to find someone to help me out with the basic management. I have a staff that cleans, and I like doing the grounds myself, so it won't be much different, just a little more hands-on time. Mayme is also resigning from her job at the library. They will have to hire a new person too."

"What about her house?" Angel asked.

"She's keeping it for the time being. She claims she needs to keep it for when my mom comes to stay so my mom doesn't take over the B&B. If Mom were staying at the B&B, I would come back to the house to all the furniture moved around, and I would find wild paintings up on my walls that don't fit with the calm of the abode. She always says when she visits that I need to wild it up."

"Whatever that means," Angel said.

"You don't want to know. Trust me." Matt stood up. "I guess I better get over to the Brick Schoolhouse and welcome my new guests who are coming late this afternoon. Do you want to come for dinner?"

"I think I'll pass and take time to get used to my new living arrangements. I might actually take some time over at the house to do some sketches and drawings so I have everything ready to go when I want to start."

"Tomorrow's Sunday. Should we attend church and then take a walk in your woods? We can bring a hatchet to make a path so we can have a picnic by the creek. I can serenade you with my charms."

Angel blushed. "The walk would be nice, and starting to clear the path would be better because I must admit, I do get a little creeped out thinking about doing it myself, because I don't know what critters might be hiding in the weeds."

"You mean a snake in the grass?"

"Yes, the slithery kind, not the two-legged kind. I'm terrified of snakes."

Matt took Angel's hand and pulled her up from the sofa. He brought her close enough to him to give her a quick peck on the lips. "A taste of the future, my lady."

Before Angel could answer back, he turned and walked out the door.

"I'm not sure about this. Are you, Blink?"

The black labradoodle looked at the door and then looked at Angel. She then jumped on Angel, knocking her off-balance back onto the sofa and began licking her face.

Angel fended off the doggy kisses. "Is that a yes or a no?"

Seeing the photo album with the two girl's pictures in it sitting on the side table, she picked it up and paged through it again. There were pictures in front of a church in Minneapolis. A young woman held a tiny baby while the other girl seemed to be about ten years old. Mom and daughter were smiling. It maybe was a baptism.

She had an idea. Looking at her watch she saw it was only one thirty in the afternoon. The mailman would by soon. Taking the album with her, she decided she would walk to the end of the driveway and wait for him. Maybe her old postman would be back and would know the family.

It was a beautiful summer day. As she neared the end of her driveway, she saw Black Cat sunning herself by the mailbox. She sat down in the grass to pet her. "Where have you been? You cannot be restricted, can you? I know that feeling. It's time for both of us to break out of our mold."

The mail truck was coming down the street, so she stood up. Ralph was the mailman delivering her mail today. She thought he probably didn't yet know the families in Whistle Stop, but it didn't hurt to ask.

"Hi, Ralph."

"Your mail," he said as he handed her a stack of envelopes.

"Can I talk to you for a minute?"

He hesitated before answering. Getting out of the vehicle, he said, "I guess so. Don't want to get behind. Date night tonight, you know." Seeing Black Cat, his eyes narrowed. "Nice cat you have here." He bent down to pet it.

Black Cat hissed and ran down the driveway.

"None too friendly, is he?"

"It's a she and has a mind of her own." Opening the photo album, she showed Ralph the pictures of the two girls and then turned to one of the ladies holding a baby by the church. "Do you recognize these people? This was in the package with just my address, no name and no return address that you delivered to me. I'm sure it was a mistake, and I want to find the owners. They may want this album with these memories. I saw these two girls recently."

"That a fact." He rubbed his chin. "Can't say that I know who they are. Can I snap a picture of the girls and ask around?"

"I guess that would be fine. You'll let me know if you find anything out."

"Have you talked to Ted Pangborn or Barney about this?"

"Barney didn't recognize them, and going to Ted is my next step. It's not as if they are lost. It's just I want to find them to give them this album."

Ralph climbed back in his truck. "I would wait on telling Pangborn. No need when it's not a police matter. This small burg doesn't get too excited about things like that. Slow as molasses this community. I might put in for a transfer. So don't be surprised if you get a new mailman again. This burg's too boring for me. Where did you say you saw those two girls again? It might help me decide which side of town to help locate the owner of the album."

"Actually, they were walking near my property. They said they are part of the rescue group that looks for the cats, but no one in the group seems to know them. Thanks for your help. Good luck with your hot date." Angel turned away to go back to her house.

"Hold up there, Angel." Charlie Mattson was puffing to catch up with her.

"Where did you come from, Charlie? You were just here this morning helping me with my move."

"I decided I needed a walk and I wanted to talk to you."

"Let's sit in the gazebo. Do you want something cold to drink?"

"No, I'm fine. The gazebo is fine."

Angel saw he was carrying something. She sat down and indicated he should sit on the wicker seat across from her. "What's that you have in your hand?"

"That's what I want to talk to you about. I haven't been quite honest with anyone here."

Angel gave him a piercing look. "Would you like to elaborate?"

He handed her what he had.

She looked at it and turned it over. "It's a book. *The Thin Red Line.* That's the book Dixon had by his side when he died. Why do you have it?"

She touched her pocket and realized she left her cell phone in her house. Glancing around, she gauged how long it would take her to get out of the gazebo, run into the house, and lock the door should she need to.

"Don't be alarmed. It's not what you think. I'm the author of this book. I'm a writer and this is my pen name. My real name is Charlie Mattson. And it's a coincidence I was here in town when the murder happened. I couldn't believe they thought my book could have triggered Dixon to kill his sister. I couldn't live with that."

"Have you told the police this and why were you here in town?"

"I haven't told the police. There was no reason for them to know I was the author of the book, and I didn't want to say anything until I knew the lay of the land, so to speak. I actually was here and interested in the house. I thought it would be a perfect place to have a weekend retreat, entertain my friends from the city, and get away to write without the phone ringing, etcetera. In Whistle Stop I could just be plain ole Charlie Mattson, but I swear it's all coincidence."

"I see. Why are you telling me this now, and why have you told no one else?"

"I would appreciate it if you could keep it quiet. I thought since Jerilyn died in the house and the circumstance of Dixon's death, you should know that I wrote the book, and I also wanted to ask you to let me write a murder mystery based on your house."

Angel frowned. "You want to write a murder mystery based on the deaths of Jerilyn and Dixon?"

"Yes and no. It would be fiction, but I'm also intrigued by the journal you found in your house. I would like to incorporate that too. I would like you to work on it with me for the foundation of the story, and you would definitely have veto power since I would be using your house and part of your find. Look up my pen name online if you haven't heard of me. You will see I'm on the up and up."

"I have heard of you, but you look different from the pictures on your cover and in real life."

Charlie laughed. "Well, the pictures we use are of me when I was much younger, and they are doctored quite a bit with different color hair and glasses. And in youth we are a little slimmer."

"How do you get away with it during book appearances?"

"I don't do them. My assistant does them and speaks for me. I'm known as the reclusive writer. I'm on a speakerphone or podcast so no one can see me, and I answer questions that way," he explained.

"Are you going to write about Orvis the ghost?" She teased him.

"Maybe, is that a yes?"

"That is a... I'll think about it."

Charlie stood up. "Fair enough. I'll be in touch."

"Are you going to continue to stay at the B&B if you do this?"

"I am for a while. I have to go back to Minneapolis for a couple of weeks next month, but then I'll be back. It'll depend on your answer how long I stay after that. I'm still looking for the right property for my writing retreats."

Angel stood up to follow him out the gazebo. "Have a good night, Charlie. I think I'll sit on my balcony overlooking the woods and have myself a glass of wine and relax. A nap might be in order too. It's been a long day."

CHAPTER THIRTY-THREE

A ngel sat on her balcony on the second floor of the carriage house, drinking a glass of wine and staring out at the trees. She thought she saw a movement deep into her woods. Maybe it was a deer. Residents said they had seen deer on her property. Sighing, she sunk back into the cushions of her chair. Should she believe Charlie? Or should she be afraid of Charlie? Who were the girls who had popped up unexpectedly on her property? She sat up and surveyed the edge of the trees. Black Cat was going back into the woods. Drat, she had better get her before she got too deep in. Blink and Magic were lounging by her side and didn't wake up when she stood.

She ran down the stairs and looked out the glass doors onto her patio. She didn't see her anywhere. She hoped the cat came back before Bridgette found her again. Bridgett didn't get that some cats, like people, couldn't be tamed and had to have the freedom to roam.

Her stomach began to growl. Instead of fixing herself a meal, she decided she would run over to the White House Eatery and get some takeout and bring it home and eat on her patio. Though a small town might be quiet, the friendliness was not something she was used to, and so it seemed there was always someone around or stopping by. She liked it, but she liked her space too.

When she opened the door, Black Cat was sitting on the step, waiting to be let in. She let out a meow and quickly ran up the stairs to the loft.

"I guess you changed your mind. Couldn't you see the trees for the forest? Or was it the other way around?" She jokingly used the old cliché, wondering if she even knew what it meant since she hadn't heard it before moving to Whistle Stop. Closing the door firmly she turned and locked the door, then chose to unlock the door, deciding to trust in the small town. She was going to take a chance even with the strange happenings.

Pocketing her keys she held her hand on the side of her pocket a little longer than necessary. *Was she becoming one of them?*

CHAPTER THIRTY-FOUR

The White House Eatery was busy. Saturday-night specials were popular with the Whistle Stop residents. Entering the eatery, she saw the homeless man sitting at the counter. He turned and saw her and then grabbed his *to-go* bag and rushed past her but not before giving her a hard look with his eyes. She wondered why she had upset him so much.

Waiting for her order at the counter, she didn't see anyone she knew. Even the waitresses were unfamiliar to her. Angel didn't linger after picking up her food since she didn't see any of her friends, although everyone gave her a friendly greeting when she passed by them.

The streets were quiet; the temperature was perfect for the start of a summer evening. She drove back into her driveway and parked her truck, picked up her food, and retreated to her house. She no more than closed her door when Black Cat rushed over and began pawing and meowing at the door. Shrugging her shoulders, she said to the cat as she opened the door, "Don't tell Bridgette I let you out, but I have a feeling you can take care of yourself." She reached down to pet the cat before she left, looking out the door at the same time she saw the homeless man coming out of the back door of her Victorian house. He looked around to make sure no one was watching, turned, and appeared to be locking the door with a key. *He had a key?*

She quickly pulled the door shut, leaving only a crack so she could peek out. Angel decided confronting him might not be safe, especially after her last encounters with him. She would check the house as soon as she was sure he'd left. Then she would call the police. Was he squatting in her house?

Seeing him skulk around the house and out of sight, she waited five minutes before leaving. Making sure she had her cell phone and her key, she walked across her yard, looking in every direction to make sure the man wasn't around watching her. Maybe she should call the police before she went in? But then she did that before, and there wasn't ever anyone there or anything missing. She would wait.

Using her key, she went inside. The light from the sun outside, though getting lower in the sky, lit up the kitchen. Everything seemed to be in place. Moving through the dining room, she noticed when she got to the living room the bathroom door was open and there was something on the floor. She flipped the switch on the bathroom light. Lying on the floor was a thermometer. Was the homeless man sick?

She moved back into the living room and saw a piece of the old heavy wainscoting was askew. *Was the man pulling the wainscoting off the wall?* She touched the wood and found it was hinged on the inside. A little push popped it open, revealing wooden stairs that led downward into the darkness. This wasn't where the basement stairs were, and there was no indication in the basement that there was a second set of stairs.

She again wondered if she should call someone, but her curiosity got the best of her and she decided she would see where the stairs went. Obviously, the homeless man knew about them, but he wasn't around.

Carefully she took a step down, stopping to turn on the flashlight on her cell phone. The steps continued downward until they reached a tunnel that actually was quite clean. Excitement began to build at finding this in her house.

Following the tunnel, she saw a light up ahead. *Did it come out somewhere on her property?* She could hear water running. *Could it be the creek?* At the entrance to the tunnel, she stopped, not believing what she was seeing.

"Who are you?" the woman said to Angel. She held a knife in front of her.

"My name is Angel Delaight and I own the property. Who are you?" Angel didn't let the fear in her voice show.

"I heard you bought the property. How did you find us?"

"Us?"

The teenage girl Angel had seen on her property stepped beside the woman.

"Please go away and leave us alone and don't tell anyone you saw us," the girl pleaded.

"Emily, go take care of your sister. Your uncle will be back soon with some medicine." The woman turned to Angel as she put the knife down. "I'm sorry, but I wasn't sure who was coming through that tunnel. I knew my brother wouldn't be back yet."

Angel came forward. "What is this? You're camping here? Why? Your brother is the homeless man who used to live with Dixon? I don't understand, and why does your brother have to get medicine?"

The woman indicated Angel should come forward and sit down on the camp chair. The woman sat down next to her. "Can I trust you?"

"I think I should be the one to ask that question." Angel looked around as she answered.

"My name is Emma. My teenage daughter is Emily, and my four-year-old is Ellie."

The children came and sat down next to their mother, and Angel acknowledged them by a smile and a nod of the head so as to not scare them.

"My children were all named after me and my mother who was Emaline." She started wringing her hands.

"How did you end up here, by my creek?" Angel asked softly, not wanting to appear to intimidate the woman in front of her children.

"We were living in the Victorian house until Mrs. Travis decided to sell it. My brother is a doctor in Minneapolis. His name is Franklin Bennet. My maiden name is Bennet. Franklin and Dixon were friends in college and kept their friendship through the years. Franklin helped me and my kids leave an abusive relationship. We moved out into an apartment of our own, but my husband kept harassing us. He threatened to kidnap the kids, and then he tried to murder me by pushing me off the balcony of the apartment building."

Angel didn't know what to say. "Why isn't he in jail?"

"He is a con artist and knows how to manipulate the system, and it was my word against his. Plus he is a former police detective. He was suspended because of a case gone badly. They said he was drunk on the job. When I went over the balcony, he told the police I had too much to drink, lost my balance, and fell. I had been drinking, but that wasn't what happened, and I was unconscious for weeks before recovering."

"And you went back with him after you were out of the hospital?" Angel's asked in disbelief.

"He had the kids and I knew I needed to go back so I could get them. After I was reunited with them, I finally pressed charges about that incident, but too much time had passed, and the system believed him. Why wouldn't they? He had been in law enforcement."

Angel glanced at the girls, who were listening to the conversation. "Are you sure we should continue this conversation in front of your daughters?"

"They know everything. They lived it with me."

Emily spoke up. "It's fine. We have no illusions about our father. Especially me. "Ellie"—she took her sister's hand—"understands too but in a different way, because she saw it all. She still loves dad and we support that, but she really doesn't understand."

"Daddy doesn't always feel well, so sometimes he loses his temper. He says it's okay, but I know it's not. I just want my daddy to get better. He loves me a lot." Ellie looked down at her feet and then laid her head in her mother's lap.

Emma continued her story. "At first in our relationship I didn't want to admit what happened. I was ashamed. When things had escalated again, I tried to leave. I didn't trust the system anymore. I got a restraining order, but he just got a slap on the wrist. It didn't matter where we went. He found us. We even tried a safe house, so Franklin decided to take matters into his own hands. I was afraid for my life and my children, and so we decided we should totally disappear for a time until we could figure out our next move."

"And the next move was camping out on my property? What's next?" Angel asked.

"We were doing well at the house. No one ever came on the property, and it's well hidden from view. The kids could play in the back. It was a warm shelter in the winter. Dixon made sure of that. He let Franklin stay under the guise of a homeless man. No one would suspect he was a doctor. When he had to go to the city to attend to his patients, Dixon would help out. They were devising a plan, and then it all fell apart."

Angel nodded in understanding. "The house was put up for sale."

"Yes. Dixon decided we could camp by the river. He knew of the tunnel because he remembered his grandfather showing him when he was a kid. He cleaned it up so it was usable. We didn't have to worry about cold weather because it was summer. When I was young, my family used to camp outside, so I thought it could be an adventure for the kids until we found a solution."

"Was it bad?" Angel asked, only having used a camper.

Emma laughed. "No, it has been fun." Black Cat joined Emma on the chair. "Midnight, you are back."

"Black Cat is your cat?"

"It's Ellie's. You call her Black Cat?"

Angel reached over to pet the cat. "We do. She has been hanging out with my new animals. She wouldn't happen to have a kitten that looks just like her?"

"No, Midnight cannot be a mother anymore. It was all we could do to get my husband to let us keep her."

"Now back to my other question. Why do you need medicine?"

"Ellie is running a fever, and I'm out of children's Tylenol. Franklin checked her out and thinks she might need some antibiotics for a throat infection. It might be viral, but just in case it gets worse, he wanted to have some antibiotics to treat her. He's going to do a strep test. He has hospital rights in a community about forty-five minutes from here. So they will do the testing for him."

"You can't stay here, especially if Ellie is sick."

"Would you let us move back to the house? We have been using the shower from time to time. Not so much so that you would notice the water bill, but if that's a problem, Franklin will pay you. And when it storms or rains, we have been staying there at night, hoping you wouldn't notice."

"This has got to stop," Angel said. "No, you are not going back to the house. You are coming to my carriage house and staying with me. I just got it finished."

"It's too dangerous. What if my husband finds us? The only one who knew about us was Dixon. I can't believe he killed his sister and then killed himself. She must have found out about us and was going to tell someone. We didn't want anyone to get hurt because of us, but I was so scared for my children. Franklin assured me he didn't believe that's what happened, but from what he said the police believe it."

Angel said, "Get your stuff together. You are coming home with me. We will figure this out. We won't tell anyone you are there. Once Ellie is feeling better, we'll make other plans."

She heard a noise behind her. Turning to investigate, she saw the homeless man coming out of the tunnel. He stopped when he saw her.

"Why are you here? I told you to leave it alone." He put himself between his sister and Angel.

"I told her the entire story, Franklin. She must have seen you leaving the house. She wants to help us."

Franklin gave Angel a shrewd look. "And how do you think you can help when I can't even help with all my connections?"

"I don't know, but this isn't the answer. At least bring them to my house until her daughter feels better," Angel pleaded.

Franklin grabbed her gently by the arm and pulled her over to the tunnel so his sister couldn't hear the conversation. "We can't put them in danger."

"How could they be in danger at my house? No one knows they're here. And everyone knows everyone in a small town. We would know if there were any strangers lurking about. You know how Whistle Stop is."

"Listen, what you don't know and what the police don't believe—because I checked it out with Ted Pangborn—is that Jerilyn and Dixon were murdered. I think Emma's husband did it because he found out they were here in town, staying in the house. I think he tried to get Jerilyn to tell him, but she couldn't tell him what she didn't know, so he killed her. Then he got to Dixon, but it didn't make sense his killing Dixon because then he couldn't learn anything, so maybe I'm off on my hunch."

"You can trust me. This is no way for them to live. You aren't thinking clearly since you are too involved," Angel pointed out.

"And you know what to do?"

Angel shook her head. "I have no idea what to do, but I do know that camping is fun, but not permanently. At least for tonight bring them back to my house and take care of Ellie. You can stay too. The Airstream is empty, or I can stay in the Airstream again. You can stay in the house with your sister, but I'm not leaving her until they come with me, and if they don't, I'll call Police Chief Pangborn and report intruders on my property, and then the authorities will take over. Do you want that? Maybe that's what I should do. I want them to be safe. This is out of my Chicago-girl league. The only thing I had to deal with in my job there were dead, homeless people."

Franklin looked back at his sister. She was nodding and there were tears in her eyes. "Fine, let's go. We'll get them back to your house, but we stay in the big house until it gets dark so no one sees them going across the yard."

Angel turned to Emma. "Get the girls. Let's get you packed up for what you will need for the next few days." She walked over and gave Emma a hug. "I don't know how, but I promise we will protect you."

Emma looked her in the eye and grabbed her so tight she almost fell over, the *thank you* coming from Emma's lips barely audible.

CHAPTER THIRTY-FIVE

A knock on the door startled the people sitting in the great room of the carriage house. Angel said, "Upstairs, everyone. Make sure you don't leave anything down here."

Emma whispered, "I was just taking this cereal up to Ellie. Come on, Emily, let's get upstairs. Hopefully Franklin will call soon with the results of the strep test."

Angel stood by the door until she made sure no one could be seen. Pulling it open, she saw Henderson standing on the doorstep. "Henderson, good morning."

"Angel, I think I found something."

"It's such a beautiful morning. I was just going to have my coffee in the gazebo. Why don't we go out there? Would you like a cup?"

Henderson shook his head. "No, I'm fine. I'm shaken up by what I found, so I came right over. I discovered it late last night and almost came over then."

Angel took her coffee and joined him outside, indicating they should walk over to the gazebo.

"You look tired. Didn't you sleep well in your new home?" Henderson asked when they reached the gazebo.

"Oh, I have a new mattress and you know how it is, always hard to get used to a new bed, and I was so excited to have the carriage house renovated."

"Look at this." Henderson thrust two documents into her hand.

"What am I looking at, Henderson?"

"I found them in Jeri's grandmother's things. They're birth certificates."

"Is it Jeri's mother's?"

"No, Jeri's mother is listed as the mother on one of them."

"Oh, is this Jerilyn's birth certificate? It must be right around her age, but the name is different. Did Jerilyn change her name?"

Henderson shook his head. "I don't think so. The date is off. This date is four years before Jeri was born."

"The name of the birth mother is Geraldine Warner. There is no father listed. It looks like the second one is a copy of the first with the name Geraldine Warner whited out and the name of a different woman written in along with the father listed. Do the names Elizabeth and Henry Talbot mean anything to you? Lily Kate. This baby was named Lily Kate. It was a girl. The girl in the carriage house, her hunch was right. She did have a girl, and she named it Lily," Angel said. "Did Jerilyn ever say anything to you about seeing this?"

"No. I don't think she knew about it. The day Jeri's mother died on the steps of the carriage house this box was lying at the foot of the steps. It appeared she was carrying it down from the upstairs when she tripped on the loose board and fell and died. We had movers transport what was left in the attic of the house and carriage house to the attic of our house after her mother died. Knowing it caused her mother's death, Jeri didn't look in the box, sealed it up, and wanted me to burn it, but I put it in our attic thinking it might hold something valuable and when Jeri was ready, she might want to open it. But Jeri never showed any interest in the box. She said she didn't want to know anything about a house and people who treated their daughter so cruelly. She didn't know the reason, just had her mother's word. I found these birth certificates in the box."

"Henderson, do you think what I am thinking? Jerilyn's mother is the person locked in the carriage house to have her baby. Jerilyn and Dixon had a sister."

Henderson hung his head. "All these years and no one knew. It would have made Jeri so happy to know there was a sister out there to add to their family. I wonder if her father knew."

"Wouldn't he have said something?" Angel asked.

"In those days if women had a baby out of wedlock, it was kept hidden. Jeri's mom might not have told him. Maybe her mom snuck into the carriage house to find the box and look for her child after the years had passed, but she never got a chance to find out where her daughter ended up. She allowed Dixon to visit her parents and Jeri too if they wanted, but she never set foot in that house from the day she married until the day she died. She wouldn't talk about it and everyone left it alone. At least that is what Jeri told me." Henderson wiped a tear from his eye. "Where do we go from here? Do I let it go?"

Angel thought for a moment. "No, I can't let this go. And I know the perfect person to help us, but I can't tell you why right now. Trust me. I have something else I have to figure out first, but maybe we will find more clues when I start on this house. After all, Jerilyn and Dixon are dead, and besides your son, there are no known relatives left, so I think we can be patient for a time. Does that work for you?" Angel glanced toward the carriage house, thinking she heard a sound.

"I'll go through the rest of the things in the attic and see if I can find anything more. Do we keep this a secret, or should we tell the others?"

"I don't think there is any reason to keep it a secret. Maybe it wasn't as much of a secret as we think it is, this being a small town."

A burst of giggles broke the silence.

"You have children visiting?" Henderson asked, looking in the direction of the house.

"It must have been a bird we heard. You know sometimes the sound is off out here."

Henderson gave her a stern look. "I wasn't born yesterday. I know a child laughing when I hear one."

Angel patted his hand. "Henderson, there is nothing I can talk about right now, and I know I can trust you when I tell you to not say anything about hearing a child giggle to anyone."

Henderson considered her request for a minute. "I can do that, but you saved my life by having me work on the carriage house. I was lost and lonely and you got me out of the house. If you're in trouble or need help with anything, you will let me know."

"I will. I promise. I just need to sort some things out."

A loud crash came from the back of the carriage house.

"I think I better go and investigate and make sure the deck didn't fall off. Remember, not a word."

CHAPTER THIRTY-SIX

"What was the crash? Was someone hurt?" Angel said as she entered the carriage house.

"No, I'm so sorry. Ellie was playing with the dog, and they both got excited and knocked the plant off the railing on the upstairs deck. As soon as we get this straightened out, I'll pay for it," Emma said. "Good news. I hope you don't mind, but I answered your cell phone when I saw my brother's number that you put in your phone last night. Ellie doesn't have strep, and she is feeling much better."

"That's good to hear." Angel mussed the hair on the Ellie's head. "You do look better."

"Is this our new home? Can Midnight come and stay too? She stays here all the time anyway. I think she likes Blink and thinks she is the black kitten's mama." Ellie looked at Angel with hopeful eyes.

"No, Ellie. This is not our home. We just came here last night because you were sick. This kind lady let us stay." Emma hugged her daughter.

Emily joined them. "Are we going back to the campground, or do we have to leave to go somewhere else?"

Emma looked at her daughter. "I'm hoping we can go back to the creek until Uncle Franklin figures something else out."

"You can't keep running," Angel said. "Do you have a picture of your husband so if we see a stranger, we will recognize him?"

"I don't. I left with nothing but what we were wearing. Franklin and Dixon provided the rest. We have to leave before someone sees us."

Angel thought for a moment. "You are not leaving. You're staying here until we get this sorted out. I don't know much about abusers except they will keep looking. What if he found you and you were by yourself? This way I'm here, and if I know the friends I have made in this community, they will be here for you too. We can make sure you are never alone and… we will get some professional advice."

"I don't think Franklin will agree to that. He wanted us to live with him in Minneapolis, and he was going to hire someone to watch us, but my husband found out and tried to break in one night before we had protection in place and Franklin was at work. Luckily a neighbor saw him and called the police before confronting the intruder. The lock was already broken and when the neighbor said the police were on the way and he would be arrested for the robbery, he ran."

"Did he assault your neighbor?" Angel asked.

"No, he made the excuse he was locked out of his brother's apartment and was just trying to get in, but he would go visit his brother at his office to get the key. He left before the police came. I talked to them and explained the situation, but there was nothing they could do," Emma explained.

"I'm going to give your brother a call and see if he might agree with me." Angel took her phone and went out to her Airstream to talk to him uninterrupted.

CHAPTER THIRTY-SEVEN

"I brought my special potato salad," Mayme said as she met Angel in front of the carriage house. "Do you want it in the house?"

"Yes, take it in and put it on the kitchen counter. Where's Dad?"

"He'll be along. He and Matt are talking about some changes Matt wants to make at the B&B. Matt's bringing cheesecake."

"And Dad?"

Mayme laughed. "He will tell you that the barbecue brisket he is bringing he made himself, but actually he got it from Our Little Secret."

Barney Pipe and Lila arrived together. Angel eyed them with speculation.

"Don't get any ideas," Lila said.

"Get ideas," Barney added.

"Barney!" Lila gently poked him in the arm. "He gave me a ride. My car wouldn't start."

"More like someone slashed the tires," Barney reminded her.

"Who would do that?" Angel asked.

"That is a good question. I must have put something on someone's autopsy that the family didn't like. Where should I put our food?"

Angel gestured toward the house.

"Chief Pangborn. I'm happy you could come," Angel said as Ted Pangborn got out of his car.

"I think this is the best plan to keep your friend safe. I don't have the resources to have someone out here all the time. Are you sure you should have included Charlie Mattson? I like the guy, but can we trust him? He seems to always be turning up at the right time, but a background check didn't find anything suspicious. Well, maybe one thing, but it wasn't important to this problem."

"I know a few things about him that you don't, or maybe you do know if you ran a background check, and I think he can maybe help us," Angel replied. "Everyone's almost here. We are waiting for Matthew, my father, Henderson Travis, and Charlie. According to Mayme, they are on their way."

Franklin Bennet came around the side of the house. Chief Pangborn gave him a keen look. "You sure clean up good. You should have come to me months ago. Maybe we could have done something sooner and your sister wouldn't have had to camp out."

"Her husband has a way of manipulating people, including law enforcement. He also has been known to change his looks so he isn't recognized. He has a friend who's a makeup artist that he used when he was undercover in his police work so he can hide in plain sight."

"Why don't we all go in and get this show on the road," Angel said. "Oh my goodness, I'm starting to talk like all of you. The rest of the party is just coming up the driveway."

The men followed her into the carriage house where the others were gathered. Conversation filled the room. Soon her father, Matthew, Henderson, and Charlie came in. When Matthew saw Franklin, he was about to say something, but Angel beat him to the punch.

"Welcome to my housewarming. I'm happy you all came. Before we begin the party, I have a favor to ask of all of you. You were all part of this project, and I found living in a small town really does mean you watch out for one another. What I'm about to say I would like kept in this room and not shared with the community. I feel I have come to be able to trust you. I'll turn this over to Chief Pangborn first."

"It's good to see all of you. Most of you I know very well and so I know you to be trustworthy and solid. Angel here has brought a situation to my attention, and since I don't have the resources to handle it without making it public, I'm going to turn to you. Please know that we don't think it is dangerous, but any of you can opt out if you want."

Matt frowned and moved closer to Angel. The rest of Angel's new friends murmured to each other.

"I would like to introduce you to Emma, Emily, and Ellie." Angel motioned to the little family that was standing on the stairs unnoticed by the group. "Emma is Franklin's sister. Franklin is not homeless but was posing as a homeless man living with Dixon so he could keep an eye on his sister and her family, who were living secretly in the Stevens' house."

"What?" Henderson Travis stood up. "You were living here without Jeri knowing? Why? Was that why Dixon didn't want to sell the house? Why didn't he just tell her?"

Franklin stepped forward. "It wasn't that he didn't trust her, but we felt the fewer people who knew the better. I'm so sorry for your loss of both of them."

Ted Pangborn spoke up. "Emma, you might want to take the kids upstairs while we finish this discussion. We will have you come down to meet everyone when we're done."

Emma nodded and ushered the kids upstairs.

Ted continued. "Emma is hiding from an abusive husband. He put her in the hospital in a coma and threatened her life. He is a former police detective and knows how to twist a situation. Until we can figure out a way to stop him or even find him, Emma needs protection."

"How sad," Mayme said. "No one should have to live like that."

Ted acknowledged her comment with a nod of agreement. "Up until now, he has been unable to find her. Dixon and Franklin were former college friends and stayed in touch all these years. Franklin is a doctor in Minneapolis. So far, Emma's husband has not found her, and I'm doing everything I can from a law enforcement perspective. Until we find a solution, Emma and her children are going to stay here with Angel in the carriage house."

Henderson stood up and said, "All this was happening right under Jeri's watch with the house? I just can't believe it." He sat back down and put his head in his hands.

Ted answered. "Unfortunately it was and it is time we solved this problem. We want to make sure there is someone with Emma and her family twenty-four seven. We don't think they will be in any danger if they are not by themselves. So far, the attacks have only been in private. If Angel goes out, she will contact one of you to see if you will help. We are not going to hide them but make sure if they are out and about in town, someone is with them."

Angel stepped forward and took over from Ted. "Keep on the lookout for new people in town—someone you don't know. A male or anyone asking questions that might appear to be about Emma. We have our suspicions that he knows where she is, because I was sent a photo book anonymously and haven't been able to find out who sent it. Are you willing to help?"

There was a buzz of conversation before Jessie stood up. "Of course."

Mayme said, "Matt, can't we use some teenage help at the B&B?"

"I guess we can. There are always people around there. In fact, they can stay there if they want."

"No, they are fine here. We can work it out," Angel said. She went over to the stairwell and hollered up, "Emma, do you want to come on down and meet your new family?"

CHAPTER THIRTY-EIGHT

"I'm going to go inside the house and start pulling the old wallpaper off the walls in the living room," Emma said to Angel. Emma had volunteered to help do what she could inside the house, so she felt better living with Angel without paying her. Plus starting on the house early would get Angel in there sooner.

Angel was sketching a garage nestled into the woods on a piece of paper so she could work up the plans to get started building. Having taken a few weeks off to get Emma and her family settled and to set up some security, she decided it was time to get back to work.

There had been no indication Emma's husband knew where they were. No strangers except for those staying at the Brick Schoolhouse had been noted in town. And Matthew made sure he vetted his guests before they arrived. Even Eudora, being aware there was a new family in town, had made sure they felt welcome, inviting them over for a meal and showing the girls her collection of antique dolls. Of course, Eudora didn't know the real story. She thought they were Angel's friends from Chicago coming to Whistle Stop to help Angel with the renovations, which is what they told everyone, careful never to mention their last names.

"That's great, Emma, but remember Orivis the ghost when you crawl on the ladder, he might try to *white* you out."

Emma laughed. "I haven't met him yet. No one has ever tried to white me out, just wipe me out. Are you sure Ellie will be okay out here with you and the furry ones?"

"I love your sense of humor. They are fine. She loves coloring while in the gazebo, and Black Cat is never far from her side. Plus she keeps an eye on Magic and Blink and herds them back when they are wandering away. We can all be outside, and I don't have to keep looking for them."

"If Bridgette brings Emily home from the Brick Schoolhouse, send her in. Those two have become fast friends. I don't ever remember Emily smiling so much." Emma gave a wave and disappeared into the house.

It was a beautiful August day, not too hot and the flowers were blooming and the grass was green. Angel could even hear the buzzing of the bees in the flowers. She raised her face to the sun and closed her eyes. It was very seldom she'd had days like this in Chicago.

A vehicle broke the silence of the morning. The mail truck was coming up her driveway. Since she was around the back of the house, the mailman wouldn't be able to see her. Thinking it was the book on Victorian house parts she ordered from an online restoration company, she didn't get up. He could leave it at the carriage house where packages usually got left. He probably wouldn't even knock to see if they were home because her truck was getting serviced at Butch's Auto Repair, and they'd locked the doors before they came out to the backyard.

She returned her attention to her sketch. Deciding she needed another angle, she walked around to the farthest side of the house away from the driveway. She thought perhaps the garage would go on the opposite side of the property from the carriage house over to the side, nestled in the trees at the edge of her yard. That way she could create a pathway from the gazebo through the trees near the carriage house and out to the creek.

She heard a giggle and lifted her head to see Ellie running around the gazebo with Blink chasing her. It brought a smile to Angel's face. What could be better than a child's laughter?

Angel heard a footstep and saw Ralph the mailman heading toward the gazebo. Something in his stride made her stand up and hurry over to block his path.

"Good morning, Ralph. What can I do for you?"

"Oh, I just saw the little one playing and wanted to say hi. I love little ones. I carry candy in the mail truck to give to the kids and treats for dogs." He held out his hand.

"I see. That's very nice of you."

Ellie ran out and stopped by Angel. She peered at Ralph with squinted eyes.

"Is that you, Daddy, under all that hair? When did you grow so much hair? And it's a different color. Can I pull your beard?"

Angel's eyes opened wide.

"Come here, Ellie. It's time to go home." Ralph reached for Ellie, but Angel blocked his arm.

In a calm voice, Angel said, "Ellie, go to your mom and tell her the door is open. Now!"

Ellie, understanding, backed away and seeing Ralph grab Angel's arm, ran to the house.

"You can't keep me from my family," Ralph yelled and pulled tighter on Angel's arm. "Come on. We are going to find them, and I'm going to take them with me."

Angel tried pulling out of his grasp as he started dragging her. Thinking quickly, Angel went totally limp and sunk to the ground to stall for time so Emma could put their plan in motion.

"I'm not going anywhere with you."

He pulled a wire from his pocket. "You don't have to. I can leave you right here. I know they are somewhere in that house."

Angel gasped. "It was you! You killed Jerilyn? Why?"

"You figured it out. She wouldn't tell me where my family was. I knew they had been hiding in this house, and I was ready to take them with me when she put the house up for sale and they disappeared. So did Franklin. I was trying to get her to tell me where they were."

"And the hidden room? How did you find it?"

"I was watching after you did your walk-through. I knew time was running out, and I confronted Jerilyn, and she did die of natural causes. I was just going to scare her with the wire. That was a great scene from that book, don't you think?"

While he was talking, Angel scanned the grounds, making sure Ellie was out of harm's way.

"I was always impressed with the method and wondered if it would work. And then she collapsed and died without telling me anything. I had watched the house, and I thought something didn't add up when I was snooping around. The perimeters of the house didn't match the rooms on the inside. When Jerilyn fell against the wall, the paneling came loose. I found the room and knew it was the perfect place to hide the body."

Angel, wanting to keep him talking to give Emma more time to get away and call the police, asked another question. "And Dixon?"

"Well, that was another matter. After Jerilyn died, I knew her brother was my next stop. I disguised my looks. I was masquerading as a woman. I make a good-looking woman if I do say so myself. My slim build makes it easy to add a few perks to my body, if you get what I mean. He was having a drink at Our Little Secret, and I befriended him."

"From what I heard, Dixon wasn't that trusting. What made him trust you?" Angel asked, thinking he was so caught up in enjoying his one-up-manship on her that he wasn't thinking about his confession. But then, if he got away with killing all of them his confession wouldn't matter. Narcissist was good way to describe this aggressor.

He laughed and got down close enough to see the fear in her eyes. "Remember these words because they may be the last ones you hear, but none of you will be able to tell anyone."

"You'd kill your own children?"

"Of course not, just you and their mother, but once I get them back we will be far away from here where no one can touch us."

"Sorry, I got sidetracked on the tidbit that you possibly would murder your children. Again, What made Dixon trust you?" Angel, staring him straight in the eye, encouraged him to talk while her hand felt around on the ground to see if she could find a rock or something sharp while he was bent down, but he broke from her gaze and stood up, staying close enough so she couldn't lift herself off the ground and make a move to get away.

"He was a ladies' man and that day I was a lady." His body shook with laughter as he remembered his ruse. "Made sure he kept drinking because I was sure I could get the information out of him. I offered to drive him home, which I did. We had a few more drinks and I was trying to get him to talk, but he passed out on me. I hoped he wouldn't remember me, but if he did when he found out his sister was dead, he might, in his foggy brain, remember a little of something. So I crushed up some sleeping medication, added it to more alcohol, and was able to wake him enough to get him to drink it, although I had to hold his jaw open to pour it down his throat. Let me tell you, I gave him enough that I knew he wouldn't wake up."

"That was taking a chance since you must have known I was coming back to my new house and I might find her." Angel had to take a little jab at him to help quell her fear. "You aren't very good at hiding bodies either."

Ignoring her taunting words, he answered, "You took your sweet time finding Jerilyn, and by the time they found Dixon, it was too late. I staged the scene, wire, book, and all, and hightailed it out of town."

"I'm sure the police will be here soon, so you better get out of here."

Ralph cackled. "It might take them a while. I think all the emergency personnel—police, ambulance, and fire—are busy at a fire at the Brick Schoolhouse B&B."

Angel gasped. "You set the bed-and-breakfast on fire?"

"I saw the package to deliver for you in the mail this morning and knew it was now or never, so I accidentally dropped a few matches on the property while I was delivering the mail on their street. It was easy walking down the street delivering mail, tossing the matches, and then leaving."

Angel began crawling backward, trying to figure out how to get out of this situation.

"Why did you send me the photo album?"

Ralph followed, flexing the wire with his gloved hands. "I wasn't sure if my family was still around here somewhere, and I thought by sending the photo album, if you didn't know where they were, you would look for the owners. You are Miss Straight and Narrow, wanting things to be right."

He had slowly trapped Angel with her back to the house and began to reach down when a loud meow pierced the air and he fell back screaming. "Ow! Get off me. Get off me."

Black Cat had attacked his back and was clawing her way to his head. He was almost successful with throwing her off when a water hose hit him square on the head with high pressure, startling him so he rolled onto his stomach, trying to shield his face. Angel scrambled away to get up. Just as she was almost to her feet, she saw a shovel come down hard on his shoulders. Emily sat on him while Bridgette tightly rolled a dog leash around his hands and arms to keep him bound.

Eyes wide, Angel stood up. "Um, wow. I guess we should call the police."

"We already did," Bridgette said. Sirens could be heard in the distance.

"Emily, I think you can get off your dad now. I'm sorry you had to be a part of this," Angel said.

Emily stood up; she had tears in her eyes. "I couldn't let him hurt you. Besides, he doesn't even look like my dad anymore and my dad isn't a nice man."

"Why don't you go and get your mother and sister and tell them it's safe. Use the door in the house. They are down by the river just like we planned if there ever was a problem," Angel said as Chief Pangborn and Barney reached them.

"Are you all okay?" Ted Pangborn said, reaching down to pull Ralph up. "Barney, take him to the hospital to check him out since it looks like his shoulder could be hurting. I'll get the story. Then take him to the station for questioning. I have a feeling we will have a lot of questions."

"Hey, boss. Come on you rootin-tootin mail shyster," Barney said as he took his prisoner's arm.

Ted Pangborn turned to Angel and Bridgette. "It appears you two are the heroes of the day. Tell me what happened."

CHAPTER THIRTY-NINE

"It feels good to be free of the worry of protecting my sister and her kids," Franklin said to Angel as they sat apart from the others, watching Ellie play with Blink and the cats.

"I can't imagine," Angel answered. "I have to admit it has been nice having them around. I'm not used to kids, so this has been an experience."

"We can look for a place for them to stay now so you can have your carriage house back for yourself."

"If they would like to stay, they can. I appreciate all of Emma's help. In fact, I want to hire her. She is pretty good at painting and details, and I could use an extra hand. I think we're going to finish off a downstairs bedroom and the bathroom first so I can move in there, and they can have the carriage house all to themselves."

"What are you two plotting? Another bad guy takedown?" Matt joined them.

"I'm so happy your B&B wasn't damaged by the fire." Angel patted Matt's hand.

"No, luckily only the garages in the neighborhood were harmed. The fire department was able to stop the fires before they got to the houses and... we had mutual aid from other local small-town departments. Without them it would have been much worse," Matt said.

"Burgers are ready," Jessie hollered from over from by the grill. Mayme stood by him, supervising.

"What are you going to do now that Mayme is branching to ranching?" Angel joked. "See, I can talk Minnesotan."

"That's Minnesotan?" Franklin scoffed.

"Actually, Emma is not only going to work for you, she is going to work for me too. Turns out she knows how to cook. I'm buying Mayme's house and going to renovate it. Emma has some ideas so eventually if things work out, she will buy it from me," Matt informed the two.

"She told me she thinks she will settle down here," Franklin said.

"Look what we found." Bridgette and Emily joined the group, handing Angel a journal.

"What is this?" Angel asked.

"I said burgers are ready!" Jessie hollered again with his spatula raised in the air.

"We better get over there," Bridgett answered. "Take a look. We found it in a secret drawer in an upstairs bedroom. Sorry we were snooping. Finding the secret room and the door to the stairs to the tunnel made us want to snoop."

Henderson invited them to join him at the picnic table on Angel's patio. "What ya got there?" He indicated the journal in Angel's hand.

Angel said, "Something the snoop sisters found." She opened the journal and started reading. "I think this belongs to you, Henderson. It's more of the puzzle."

"A puzzle? We have another puzzle?" Lila joined them. "Can I autopsy it?"

"What is it?" Henderson asked.

"It looks like it's a journal by the same young woman who was kept in the carriage house. But this looks like it was before her confinement because she is very in love here. Maybe we can get some more clues as to who it is and who the father of the baby was." Angel handed the journal to Henderson.

He pushed it back at her. "You keep it. You might find more and then you can put the pieces together. I'll keep looking through the attic."

"Hey there, folks, can I join you?" Barney plunked himself right down between Lila and Henderson, almost making Henderson slide off the bench. "How do. Lila?"

"I do very well, Barney. Thank you."

"I think I have attended more picnics here than in my entire life," Angel remarked, looking at all her new friends roaming the yard.

"I hear ya got a picnic going here," Eudora hollered as her wheelchair sped down the driveway toward them.

"I can't believe I forgot to invite her." Angel stood up.

"No worries there, girly." Charlie Mattson walked up to the group. "Haven't you learned? I have. It doesn't matter because they just know. It's a small town."

EPILOGUE

"What are you doing over here in the gazebo all by yourself, Charlie?" Angel asked as she joined him.

"Pondering my future."

Angel nodded in understanding, waiting for him to continue.

"Words are powerful things. I've always known that, but to know some words I wrote were used for evil makes me look at the words I write which might influence people's lives."

"It wasn't your fault your book was used as an idea for bad things, and you couldn't have known what would happen," Angel reminded him.

"No, but we all have a responsibility in what we say and a choice in how we influence others. I found some secluded property down by the lake, and I'm going to live there and start a writer's retreat. I want to teach other writers about the power of words and the responsibility they have when they use them."

"You are staying. Starting that retreat might let everyone in town know who you really are. You might not be able to be plain ole Charlie anymore," Angel reminded him.

"Maybe or maybe not. I have decided I'm going to write one more book and use my real name. That is, if you will help me."

"Me? I'm a contractor, a carpenter, how can I help?"

"You can let me tell the story of a young woman locked away in a carriage house in a time when teen pregnancy was taboo; a hidden life no one would know about if you wouldn't have found it. It's your choice to keep it here, quiet and still hidden away, or let me give the gift of understanding to the world. I want to give life to a house whose secrets kept a family safe from an abusive husband. I can feel it, there is more to come with that journal the girls found today. You can let me tell the real stories that might make a difference and keep someone safe or change someone's life."

Angel was silent for a moment, remembering the words from the journal of the unknown young woman in the attic. "I think I like that idea."

"Maybe while you are fixing the big house, you might find more clues as to what happened to the baby. I would love that for an ending for my book."

"Charlie, you amaze me with your insight." Angel gave him a quick hug.

Charlie looked into her eyes. "It's time I settled down. It's time I made my writing count. This experience has made me see that. I've been single a long time." He joked. "It could be my girly attitude. You've taught me that too."

They heard laughter coming from the carriage house.

"That's what should be on this property, the sound of laughter and love and children," Angel said.

"You know I'm too old for you or I would court you. Is that what they call it nowadays? But I think there are a few good men left in this world who won't call you girly."

Angel gazed into his eyes, studying the expression while he said those words. "Maybe you have learned that words count." Angel looked over to where Matthew was playing in the yard with the kids. "But I have learned that love knows no age and the heart is sometimes fickle."

"So what are you saying?" Charlie was about to say girly when he stopped and laughed with Angel, she too realizing the words he kept from saying.

"I'm saying right now my heart belongs to renovating my house. Look how old she is. We'll tell her story, and time will take care of the rest."

AFTERWORD

A LITTLE HISTORY OF WELLS DEPOT

The city of Wells was plotted in 1869 by a group of men including Clark W. Thompson, President of the Southern Minnesota Railway (SMRR). The first steam engine and a train of cars reached Wells in January 1870. The community was built around the railroad.

The depot on the cover of this book was built in 1903. It was not the first depot, but in 1899 the Chicago, Milwaukee, and St. Paul Railroad would spend two million dollars for permanent improvements and a new depot. According to former depot agent Ray Burnett, the community once had six passenger trains arriving daily.

Full passenger service ended in the late 1920s; the Doodlebug passenger train ran two trains daily into the 1950s. The building was used for an office and storage space until 2005 when the ICE/DME Railroad announced their decision to demolish the then in disrepair

Old Milwaukee Railroad depot in order to build a larger garage and office.

Members of the community rallied, and the Wells Historical Society was reborn. The city purchased the depot for one dollar, and a city resident offered the land adjacent along the railroad tracks. A combination of grants, donations, and fund-raisers restored the building, which is listed in the National Register of Historic Places. The Wells Depot Museum opened to the public in 2010.

Over the span of 150 years, numerous rail companies have owned the tracks that run through Wells and alongside the Wells Depot Museum. Currently the track is the property of the Canadian Pacific Railroad.

The whistle of the train has sounded across the prairies in the Wells area since January of 1870. Wells began as a railroad town, and so it is today, 150 years later.

Visit http://www.wellsdepotmuseum.com/ to see the restoration.

Information excerpts were taken from *To Those Who Came Before: Celebrating 150 Years of the Wells Community,* by the Minnesota Historical Society and the Wells Depot Museum.

ABOUT THE AUTHOR

As human beings, we are always a work in progress. From birth to death we live, hurt, laugh, cry, feel, and with all those emotions we grow as people, as family members, and as friends. Julie is a dreamer and feels blessed to have the opportunity in her writing to pass those dreams on to others. She believes you are never too old to dream and to turn those dreams into a creative endeavor.

Julie is the author to two cozy mystery series and a children's series. She also dabbled a bit in watercolor painting and hopes to eventually add pictures to her children's book series, *Granny's In Trouble*.

#ASmallTownCanBe #Murder is the first book in her new Whistle Stop series. She is also collaborating with the photographer in this book on a line of greeting cards to be released sometime in 2020.

You can find Julie at
http://julieseedorf.com

ALSO BY JULIE SEEDORF

THE FUCHSIA, MINNESOTA, SERIES

Granny Hooks a Crook

Granny Skewers a Scoundrel

Granny Snows a Sneak

Granny Forks a Fugitive

Granny Pins a Pilferer

Granny Bricks a Bandit

THE BRILLIANT, MINNESOTA, SERIES

The Penderghast Puzzle Protectors

The Discombobulated Decipherers

CHILDREN'S BOOKS

Whatchamacallit? Thingamajig?

Snicklefritz